SEAL's Honor

Take No Prisoners Series

Book #1

Elle James

New York Times Bestselling Author

Take No Prisoners Series
SEAL's Honor (#1)
SEAL's Desire (#2)
SEAL's Embrace (#3)
SEAL's Obsession (#4)
SEAL's Proposal (#5)

From the Author

As a retired member of the armed forces, whose father was a career military man and whose sister and brother also served, I'd like to thank all the brave soldiers, sailors, airmen, SEALs, Coast Guard and special forces who are serving or have served and sacrificed to defend this great nation.

Please take the time to thank those who have served for their commitment and dedication to keeping us free and safe.

I'd like to dedicate this book to those who made the ultimate sacrifice of their lives and to the wounded warriors who so bravely face new challenges.

If you've enjoyed this story, please consider taking the time to leave a review on your favorite retail or reader review site. Authors appreciate your thoughts about the books you read and love it when you share them with others.

Enjoy!
Elle James
aka Myla Jackson

Chapter One

Reed Tucker, Tuck to his buddies, tugged at the tie on his U.S. Navy service dress blue uniform, and his gut knotted as he entered the rehabilitation center of the National Naval Medical Center in Bethesda, Maryland.

He'd never run from anything, not a machine gun pinning his unit to a position, a fight where he was outnumbered, or an argument he truly believed in. But the sights, smells, and sounds inside the walls of the rehabilitation center made him want to get the hell out of the facility faster than a cat with its tail on fire.

But he couldn't leave. Not yet. This was graduation day for Reaper, aka Cory Nipton, his best friend and former teammate on SEAL Team 10. Reaper was being released from the rehabilitation center after enduring something even tougher than BUD/s training, the twenty-four week Basic Underwater Demolition/SEAL training designed to weed out the true SEALs from the wannabes.

But Reaper's release from rehab wasn't the only event that brought Tuck there that day. He was going to a wedding. His heart twisted, his palms grew clammy, and he clutched the ring box in his left hand as regret warred with guilt, creating a vile taste in his mouth.

Reaper was marrying Delaney, the only woman

Tuck had ever trusted with his heart. The only woman who'd forced him to get over his past and dare to dream of a future. She was the woman he could see himself spending the rest of his life with. And today she was promising to love, honor, and cherish his best friend—a better man than Tuck by far. A hero who'd lost his right arm because Tuck hadn't given him sufficient cover. Cory deserved all the happiness he could get after being medically discharged out of the only family he'd ever known. The Navy SEALs.

His hand on the door to the room where the wedding was to take place, Tuck squared his shoulders and stepped into his future.

Two months earlier

Tuck glanced to his left and right. The members of Strike Force Dragon sat or stood, tense, holding onto whatever they could as the MH-60M Black Hawk dipped into the valley between two hilltops, less than a click away from the dark, quiet village. The only thing different about this mission was that, since the one before, he'd slept with the Pilot in Command of the helicopter.

Most men knew her as Razor, the call sign they used for the only female pilot flying infiltration and extraction missions for the 160th Special Operations Aviation Regiment (SOAR), Army Captain Delaney O'Connell.

Through his NVGs he picked up the bright green signature of a lookout on top of one of the buildings.

Within seconds, shots were fired at them, tracer rounds flaring in the dark. The helicopter remained just out of range of the man's rifle shots, but it wouldn't be long before a Taliban machine gunner with long-range capability was alerted with the potential of lobbing rocket-propelled grenades their way.

Wasting no time, the helicopter sank to a level just above the drop zone (DZ). While it hovered the men fast-roped down.

As soon as his boots hit the ground, Tuck brought up his M4A1 in the ready position and ran toward the sniper on the rooftop, zigzagging to avoid being locked in the enemy crosshairs.

Reaper, Big Bird, Gator, Fish, and Dustman spread out to the sides and followed.

When they were in range, Reaper took a knee and employed his uncanny ability as a sharpshooter to knock off the sentry on the rooftop.

The team continued forward into the walled town, going from building to building, until they reached the one they were after. In the center of the compound, high walls surrounded one particular brick and mud structure.

Big Bird bent and cupped his hands.

Tuck planted his boot in the man's massive paws and, with Big Bird's help, launched himself to the top of the wall, dropping down on the other side in a crouch. Weapon pointing at the building, finger on the trigger, Tuck scanned the courtyard for potential threat. People moved past windows inside. So far, no one had stepped outside to check out the disturbance. Only a matter of time. "Clear," he said into his headset.

As Dustman topped the wall, a man emerged from the side of the structure and fired on them.

Without hesitation, Tuck fired off a silent round, downing the man with one bullet.

Dustman dropped to the ground beside him and gave him a thumbs up, taking the position by the wall so Tuck could move to the corner where the dead man lay.

As they'd discussed in the operations briefing, they only had three minutes to get into the compound, retrieve their target, and get out. Kill anyone in the way, but bring out the target alive.

Once four of the six-man team were inside the wall, they breached the doorway and entered, moving from room to room. If someone or something moved, they had only a millisecond to decide whether or not to shoot.

Tuck opened the first room. Inside, small green heat signatures glowed in his NVGs. Children sleeping on mats on the floor. He eased shut the door, jamming a wedge in the gap to keep them from getting out too soon.

He moved on to the next room. When he opened the door, a woman rose from a pallet, wearing a long black burka. When she lifted her hand like she held a gun, Tuck fired, taking her down before she could pull the trigger.

As he continued in the lead position down the narrow hallway, Tuck's adrenaline hammered blood through his veins and honed his senses. His wits in hyper-alert status, his finger rested a hair's breadth away from again pulling the trigger. This was the life he was made for. Defending his country, seeking out his enemies and destroying them with a swift, deadly strike. His job was risky, dangerous, and deadly.

A man emerged from a room down the hall.

Tuck's nerves spiked. He had only a fraction of a second to identify him.

Not his target.

He pulled the trigger and nailed him with another silent round. The man slumped to the floor, his cry for help nothing more than a startled gasp.

The door he'd emerged from flew open and men bearing guns poured out.

Tuck spoke quietly into his headset. "Get down." He didn't bother to look back. His team would follow his orders without hesitation. He dropped with them, his M4A1 in front of him, and fired at the kneecaps of the men filling the hallway.

One by one, they went down, discharging their weapons, the bullets going wide and high.

In Pashto, the language spoken by most of the population of Afghanistan and Pakistan, Tuck told them to lay down their weapons.

When one of the injured enemies sat up and took aim, Tuck fired another round, putting him out of the game.

The injured enemy soldiers threw down their guns.

"Gator, clean up out here," Tuck whispered into his mic. "Reaper and Big Bird, you're with me."

In the lead, Tuck stepped around the fallen Taliban and entered the room in a low crouch, ducking to the right. Nothing moved. Another door led into yet another unknown space. Tuck dove into the room and rolled to the side, weapon up.

As he entered, a man with an AK47 fired off a burst of rounds that whizzed past Tuck's ears, missing him, but not by much. The man shouted for Tuck to drop his weapon.

Tuck fired at the shooter's chest. He fell to the ground, revealing the man he'd been protecting. Their target, the Taliban leader they'd been briefed on. He stood straight, a pistol aimed at Tuck.

Though he wanted to pull the trigger, Tuck couldn't shoot. His mission was to bring him out alive.

His hesitation cost him. A round, fired pointblank, hit him in the chest and flung him backward to land on his ass. If not for the armor plate protecting him, he'd be a dead man. He lay still for a moment, struggling to regulate his breathing.

Reaper used the stun gun, firing off a round that hit dead on and had the man flat on his back and twitching in seconds. "You okay?" He extended his hand to help Tuck to his feet.

"Yeah." Tuck motioned to Big Bird. "Take him."

The biggest, strongest man of the team, Big Bird lifted their target and flung him over his shoulder.

Still fighting to catch his breath, Tuck led the way back to the fence. Once outside the building, he scanned his surroundings and then checked back up at the top of the roof. No signs of enemy snipers. But that didn't mean they were in the clear. They still had to navigate their way out of town and get back to the helicopter.

Leading the way, with Gator and Fish guarding the rear, Tuck hurried back along the narrow street to the outer walls of the village where the helicopter hovered nearby, waiting for their signal.

Tuck blinked the flashlight outfitted with a red lens at the hovering aircraft and it moved in, setting down for the briefest of moments, enough to get the six-man team inside. He reached over the back of the seat to the pilot and shouted, "Go!"

The Black Hawk lurched into the air, rising up and moving forward at the same time, hurrying to gain as much altitude as possible as they disappeared into the night sky, out of enemy sight and weapons range.

Not until they were well out of reach did Tuck release the breath he'd been holding and take stock of his team and their prisoner. All of them made it out alive and intact. That's the way he liked it. He'd been the only one who would have sustained injury if he hadn't been equipped with armor plating.

The co-pilot handed Tuck an aviation headset and he slipped it on.

"Nine minutes, twenty-five seconds." Gunnery Sergeant Sullivan's raspy voice sounded in Tuck's ear. "Better, but still not fast enough."

This had been a training mission, one they'd repeated five times in the past two weeks. Someone wanted them to get it right. The team was improving, but still needed to be quieter, faster, and more aware when the mission was real. The people they'd shot tonight had only been tagged with lasers. If this mission went live, the ammunition used against them would be live rounds.

Leaning back, Tuck held up nine fingers for his team to see and understand the repercussions of wearing out their welcome in a Taliban-held village.

The men nodded. Noise from the rotors precluded talking inside the chopper. When they got back to the base at Little Creek, Virginia, they'd debrief before being dismissed for the night and hitting the club.

They'd played the same scenario five times, improving with each iteration. All six members of the team were highly skilled Navy SEALs. The cream of the crop, the most highly disciplined officers and enlisted men from the Navy.

Like Tuck, the team was tired of playing pretend. They wanted to get in and do the job. But, like most missions, they didn't know when they would go, who their target would be, or where they'd have to go to take him out. Only time and their commanding officers would tell. Only when they were about two hours out would they get their final orders and all the details.

In the meantime, they'd be off duty until the following morning's PT, unless orders came in that night. It happened. But if Tuck waited around his apartment for it to come about, he'd go stir-crazy. Besides, he wanted to see O'Connell and pick up where they'd left off the night before.

Back at base, Delaney O'Connell climbed out of the pilot's seat and grabbed her flight bag. Adrenaline still thrumming through her veins, she knew going back to her apartment for the night wasn't an option.

Her co-pilot, Lt. Mark Doggett, aka K-9, fell in step beside her. "The team's headed to DD's Corral for a beer and some dancing. I know you don't usually like to hang out, but it's been a tough week. Wanna go?"

"Sure," she said, a little too quickly. Any other time, she'd have cut him off with a quick, but polite, *no*. But if she went back to her apartment alone, Tuck might show up and what good would that bring? Somehow, she'd fallen off the abstinence wagon with a vengeance and she was having a hard time getting back on.

"Great." K-9 cleared his throat. "Do you need a ride?"

"No, thank you. I prefer to drive myself."

"Probably a good idea. These Navy guys work hard and play harder."

As well she knew. Tuck had played her in bed like a musician played an electric guitar, hitting every one of her chords like a master.

Her body quivered with remembered excitement, her core heating to combustible levels. Maybe going to the club was a bad idea. If Tuck was there...

She squared her shoulders. They didn't call her Razor for nothing. She would cut him off like she'd done so many others who'd tried getting too close. And soon. Walking away from a physical relationship was a hell of a lot easier than walking away from an emotionally involved one. Delaney refused to invest her emotions in another man with an addiction to adrenaline rushes. She'd been there once and would not go there again.

Before Tuck, she'd gone two years without a man in her life. Two years since Mad Max, Captain Chase Madden, bought it on a leadership interdiction mission in Pakistan. When a Special Forces soldier had been left behind, he'd gone back into hostile territory against his commanding officer's order. His helicopter had been shot down. Max had been injured, but was still alive until the Taliban found him and dragged him through the streets tied to the back of a truck. By the time they untied him, he'd bled out.

Delaney had been devastated. No one knew she and Mad Max had gotten engaged two weeks prior to his deployment. And no one would, if she could help it. Being a part of the 160th Special Operations Aviation Regiment was an honor she took very seriously.

She understood her position was precarious. On more than one occasion, her CO had told her she was on probation as the only female ever entrusted with the honor of flight leader in an all-male corps. The powers that be were watching her every move. One misstep and she would be out, and she'd worked too damned hard to get here. Three years of training, and working her way up the food chain, and a rock-hard body, at least where it counted, had gotten her noticed.

Fooling around with Tuck, one of the Navy SEALs assigned to this training mission, wouldn't go over well with her commander. But the strain of anticipation and the long bout of celibacy had taken their toll on Delaney. She'd needed a release. When Tuck and Reaper offered to help her change her flat tire, she never dreamed she'd end up in bed with one of them. But those damned SEALs with their massive biceps and quads...

Holy shit. What a mistake. And Tuck would probably think their liaison meant something.

Which it didn't.

She didn't need a man in her life. Not when her missions were as dangerous as they were. And a relationship with a SEAL was as dumb as it got. Her in the Army, him in the Navy. Both deployable at a moment's notice and most likely to opposite ends of the earth. Only Kismet was what brought them together at Little Creek, Virginia, to train for a possible mission. If they deployed together, their sleeping together would only complicate matters. And she needed a clear head to complete the missions she would be responsible for flying.

Tonight, she'd tell Tuck not to expect anything. She wasn't into commitment or the long-term relationships.

Chapter Two

Tuck lurked in the hallway outside the ladies' room, waiting for Delaney to emerge.

When she stepped out, he snagged her arm, pulling her into the shadows at the end of the hall and into his tight embrace.

At first stiff, as soon as she realized who it was, she semi-melted into him, her body fitting perfectly against his. "Damn it, Tuck, you scared the crap out of me." She batted his arm and stared up, her brow twisted into a tight frown. "You can't go around grabbing me."

He grinned. "Kiss me."

"No."

"Then I'll have to kiss you."

"What part of no—"

Almost a full foot taller than the petite, perfectly packaged helicopter pilot, Tuck bent to close the distance, sealing her mouth with his and cutting off her argument. Loving the feel of her warm, full lips against his, he clamped his arms around her and lifted, wrapping her legs around his waist and spinning her until her back was against the wall. He deepened the kiss, thrusting his tongue past her teeth and whipping down the length of hers in a long sexy slide.

For a full fifteen seconds, she resisted, her hands pressing against his chest. Then her fingers curled into his shirt and she kissed him back. Not gently, but like she'd gone without food for a week and was hungry for him, her mouth working over his, devouring him.

God, she tasted so good, like peaches and rum. Sweet, tangy, and devilishly intoxicating.

When he broke for air, she leaned her head to the side. "I swore I wouldn't do this again."

"Why?" Tuck trailed kisses down the line of her exposed neck. He paused at the base of her throat where her pulse thrummed like the patter of machine gun bullets—fast, furious, and adrenaline-pumping. He liked it when he made her excited.

"Whatever this is between us has to end," she insisted, even as her thighs tightened around his hips.

"Why now?" Tuck slid his hand down her arm, skimming the side of her breast. The nipple beneath her T-shirt puckered temptingly. His cock hardened in response. Where she'd been hesitant to start something physical with him, in the end, she'd flown at him like she couldn't get enough.

He thought once would be enough with Delaney. That once had lasted all night and through not two but three orgasms. She'd come so readily, she had to have been denying herself for a very long time.

They both knew the relationship wasn't meant to last. Not in their line of business. Members of elite forces that could be mobilized at a moment's notice didn't get involved. It never worked. But that shouldn't stop them from grabbing a little physical release between deployments.

Tuck was all for physical release with no

emotional ties. He told women at the start of sex it was purely physical. Don't expect him to call or ever see her again. Some were okay with that. Some others, not so much. He'd walked away with no regrets.

Until he'd met Delaney. She'd pretty much echoed his stance on relationships. Don't ask for more. It would not be forthcoming.

"What about Cory? The three of us have been pretty tight these past couple of days."

They'd hung out at Cory's apartment on several occasions, drinking beer, watching sports, and scarfing down pizza. Just this morning, Cory had mentioned he could really see himself with Delaney on a regular basis. A twinge of guilt tugged at Tuck's conscience. He'd never kept anything from Cory. He was the brother he'd never had growing up. "Cory will get over it."

"And if he finds out we've taken our friendship to another level?"

Tuck's jaw tightened. "He's a big boy. He can take it." His hand slid beneath Delaney's shirt, rising toward her breast.

"Did you know he asked me out on a date?"

Tuck's hand stopped short of her bra and he straightened, eyes narrowing. A stab of something intense ripped through him. He felt an odd sense of wanting to pound his chest and roar that this woman was his. But he knew that wasn't so. "When?"

"Last night." She bent to capture his lip between her teeth, pulling on it, then sucking it into her mouth.

He drew away. "Was that the call you got while

14

we were in your shower?" He'd just lathered her up, soap sliding over her breasts and down her belly to catch in the soft curls over her mound. Damned if he wasn't feeling the need to shower again.

She nodded, trailing her finger from his lips down his throat to the collar of his shirt, loosening one of his buttons. "I told him I was busy."

His lips quirked upward. "With me."

"I didn't tell him *what* I was busy doing."

"Doing me."

"Yeah, but we both know it can't go on." Her head jerked up when a woman entered the hallway, headed for the bathroom. "And I don't want anyone to know about us." Delaney worried her bottom lip as she trailed a finger along his cheek and across his lips.

Tuck loved it when she chewed on her lip. He bent to catch that lip between his teeth, tugging gently. "We can keep this our secret."

She captured his face between her palms, her brows drawing together. "No more secrets. We need to end this."

"Coward." He smoothed the hair behind her ears, then pressed a kiss to her earlobe.

"No, really." Her words were saying one thing, while her breasts rubbed against his chest, her fingers sliding over his shoulders. "We can't keep doing this."

"We both agreed this relationship was temporary." Though he wasn't as sure now as he had been going into it. He liked being with her more than he cared to admit.

"Yes, but..."

He kissed away her 'but'. "And *you* have no

intention of making our relationship permanent, as you emphatically stated the first night we made love."

"Right." She drew her finger across the top of his ear. "As did you. And what was it you said? Ah yes, when a woman gets too close, you walk away."

He nodded. The thought of walking away from Delaney sat like sour apples in the pit of his belly. What was it about this woman that made him want to break all of his self-imposed rules? He couldn't think past the feeling of her riding him, even fully clothed. "If we're both in agreement we won't ask for permanency, then why end it now?"

"And if one of us changes his or her mind and wants more?"

There she went again, biting on her lip, driving him insane. His cock grew impossibly harder beneath the confines of his Levis. "We nip it in the bud." He bent to nibble her full lower lip, pressing down her hips, rubbing his crotch against the smooth silk of her panties.

"Understood." She laid her hands on his chest and pushed. "Let me down."

With more restraint than he knew he had, he gripped her arms. "Okay." For a moment he held her there, enjoying the warmth of her body against his.

"We both know that adrenaline junkies make terrible partners." Her hand remained on his chest. "And you, Tuck, are an adrenaline junkie."

He nodded. "I am. It's kind of a requirement of the job."

"I know." She smiled up at him, her lips a little too tight. "And if we see each other anymore than we have, I might break my promise to myself."

His chest swelled at the thought that she was worried about falling for him. "And that's a problem?"

"Yes." She pushed away and stood at arm's length. "I refuse to give my heart to someone who could die on each mission." A shadow crossed her face, her green eyes darkening.

"Honey, nothin's gonna happen to me. I'm freakin' Superman." He reached out to take her back in his arms.

"And I'm not going to be your kryptonite." She moved out of reach. "Let's just end this now. We were better off when we were only friends."

Chest tightening, Tuck realized he didn't want to end what they'd only just started. Being friends without touching her would be impossible. Anger spiked. The urge to take her, right there in the hallway, to show her how much he cared and wanted to be with her nearly overwhelmed him, almost made him lose control. He never lost control.

Tuck schooled his face into a mask of indifference. After several deep, calming breaths, he nodded. If this was the way she wanted it, so be it. He'd let her stew in her very sexy, musky juices for a little while and see if she was singing the same tune later.

"Okay, then. It ends here." His groin tight, his jeans tighter, he lifted her, pressing her back against the wall. He brushed one last, brief kiss across her soft lips and let her feet touch the ground, though he kept her pinned to the wall for a moment longer, prolonging the torture. Then he left her standing in the hallway and returned to the bar room, searching for the second prettiest girl in attendance. He had some dancin' to do, and maybe seeing him in action would get under one helicopter pilot's pretty skin.

As a U.S. Army Aviation Captain of the esteemed 160th Aviation Regiment "Night Stalkers", Delaney O'Connell, could fly her MH-60 Black Hawk into Afghanistan's Taliban-held Provinces under enemy fire without batting an eyelash, her hand firm on the controls. But when faced with creepy-crawly bugs, she squealed and went all girly on him.

And he loved it. It had taken a spider in her bathtub to get her to let him past the front door of her apartment. She'd been a tough nut to crack, refusing to be anything but friends with soldiers, sailors, and SEALs on assignment for temporary training duty with Special Operations Forces stationed at the Joint Expeditionary Base in Little Creek, Virginia.

At first, Tuck hadn't considered dating the hotshot pilot, preferring to stick to civilian women, safe from the no-fraternization rules imposed by his command and the U.S. Military. Safe, too, because when he left, transferred, deployed, or otherwise moved on, they stayed behind. His commitment was never to a woman, but to his team.

Until Delaney.

Oh, he'd still take a bullet for any one of his brothers at arms, but lately he'd had difficulty seeing himself leaving Delaney behind. And if the current TDY was any indication, as part of the joint task force, they'd trained together and would deploy together should they be called to do so.

The thought of Delaney deploying still left him feeling strange. Knowing she'd fearlessly fly into enemy-held territory didn't sit well with the protector in him. What if she was shot down? They were all members of the U.S. military, sworn to serve and protect their great nation. As a man born and raised on a west Texas ranch, Tuck had learned to respect women, treat them well, and protect them from harm. How could he do that if she was flying straight into hell?

As his grandmother always told him, *don't borrow trouble*.

Hopefully, the joint task force wouldn't be called up anytime soon. SEAL Team 10 had been deployed a couple times to various missions in the Middle East without the assistance of the 160th Special Operations Aviation Regiment squadron. And as much as he would miss Delaney on that kind of mission, he hadn't been distracted with worry over her.

Which was ridiculous. He'd told her from the start, anything he felt for her would be purely physical.

He'd been wrong.

And now, instead of him backing out of the relationship as was his modus operandi, *she* was calling it all off. Normally, that suited him fine. But this was Delaney, and she'd managed to sneak under his protective barrier, somewhere between pizza, football, and night training missions.

He glanced back as she slipped into the semi-darkness of DD's Corral, the country western nightclub frequented most by members of the units conducting joint training exercises in the Little Creek-Ft Story area for the past two months.

His member straining against the fly of his jeans, Tuck edged toward the dance floor, making his way through the crowd of men and women in civilian clothing, just as one of his favorite Tim McGraw songs struck up the first chords on the juke box.

An Army guy stood and swayed in front of Delaney. "Hey, honey, wanna dance with me?" His voice carried loud and clear as the song hit a lull in the melody.

Tuck's fists clenched and he took a step toward the two.

"Not interested." Delaney tried to get around the man.

Again, he stepped in front of her. "Ah, c'mon. Just one dance."

The man next to him jabbed an elbow in his friend's gut. "Watch out, that's Razor, the one I told you about."

"Razor, is it? You're pretty for a razor. Tell ya what, I'll bring the shaving cream, and, darlin', you can shave me any day."

Her eyes narrowed. "Still not interested." She ducked around him and moved on. Before the army guy could catch up, she grabbed the biggest Navy SEAL on Team 10, Benjamin Sjodin, and headed for the dance floor.

Nicknamed Big Bird, the SEAL was the largest

and youngest member of their team and as graceful as his Sesame Street namesake. Still, Delaney painstakingly set out to teach the man how to two-step. A farm boy from Indiana, he'd been nicknamed Big Bird because he walked like an ostrich, all lanky, jerky and unnatural, but he got the job done. Not so much on the dance floor. He stumbled and stepped on Delaney's feet and his freckles glowed every time he blushed.

"O'Connell might have the reputation of being a razor, but she also has the patience of a saint." Cory Nipton, aka Reaper, grinned. "That's the fifth time Big Bird stomped her foot. I'm keeping count."

"He has the grace of a bull in a tutu. Whatcha drinkin'?" Tuck sat on a barstool beside his friend.

Reaper lifted his bottle of Guinness and swished the liquid inside. "I'm good for now."

Tuck wasn't. He ordered another Bud from the tap, waited for the bartender to slap the mug on the counter, then took a long swallow. He needed the liquid encouragement before launching himself out into the sea of women looking for a little fun on the dance floor.

Before Delaney, he'd enjoyed dancing with just about any woman willing to put up with his less-than-stellar two-step. Since Delaney, he found himself comparing every woman to her. They didn't fit right against his body, the perfumes they wore weren't as enticing as the fresh scent of Delaney's skin. They didn't laugh like she did at his crude jokes or point out when he was being an ass. If he was honest with himself, Delaney had ruined him for other women and that went against his promise to himself to remain unhitched, unattached, and single for the duration of his military career…if not longer.

Tuck's only experience with marriage was when his mother had run out on his father and left him to deal with the old man's foul-tempered upbringing.

Not like he wanted to marry Delaney now. But he would like their relationship to last at least one more night. Maybe two. She fit him like a glove. A warm, wet glove he could drive himself into again and again.

Fuck. He'd never be able to dance if he had a hard on. He took another swallow of his beer before again facing the dance floor, scanning for a pretty woman to partner with. Maybe she'd make Delaney rethink her desire to call an end to their crazy, mad lovemaking that never should have happened in the first place. But now that it had, he wanted it to happen again.

He took in the ladies sitting at the tables, smiling and laughing, touching their hair and generally trying to appeal to the bar's male population in hope of enticing one to dance.

There was a blond with pretty hair. After a closer look, Tuck shook his head. She smiled with a big toothy grin, like she was trying too hard. The brunette beside her was passable, but she laughed too loud and often. No. He couldn't do that to himself.

One after another, he ruled out the women seated around the dance floor, his gaze shifting back to Delaney.

She laughed up at Big Bird, the musical sound

hitting Tuck square in the chest.

He jumped up from his seat.

"Where ya goin'?" Reaper asked.

"Gonna find me a woman." He stalked toward the pretty redhead at the end of the bar. "Wanna dance?"

"Sure." She grinned, slid off her seat, and stood on leopard-patterned stilettos that matched her leopard, skin-tight skirt.

Yeah, she'd do. Without waiting for her to get her bearings, Tuck grabbed her hand and wove through the tables to the hardwood dance floor. He turned and spun her into his arms, executing a perfect two-step.

Thankfully, she was graceful enough to keep up as he whisked her around, passing Delaney who struggled to keep her feet from being crunched under Big Bird's size thirteens.

When she glanced across at him, he made a point to smile down at his partner for the first time and laugh, though the redhead hadn't said a thing.

The woman he was dancing with cleared her throat to get his attention. "Don't you want to know my name?"

Not really. He gritted his teeth. "What is it?"

"Lisa." Another few steps in the dance and she raised her brows. "And your name?"

"Tuck."

Big Bird chose that moment to dip Delaney, nearly dropping her on the floor.

Tuck lurched toward them, stepping on Lisa's foot in the process.

"Ouch." Lisa leaned on his arm and limped for a moment on her injured foot.

"Sorry." He held her steady until she'd wiggled her toes and nodded.

"I'm okay."

Big Bird pulled Delaney back up in his arms and hugged her.

His jaw tightened. The caveman in him wanted to stomp across the floor, throw Delaney over his shoulder, and take her back to his cave where he'd make her his. Damn the woman for getting under his skin.

Lisa, her brow puckered, stopped in the middle of the floor, pulling Tuck to a halt. "I get it."

"You get what?" he asked, impatient for the delay when Delaney and Big Bird moved to the other end of the floor.

She planted a hand on her hip. "You're trying to make someone jealous, aren't you?"

"I don't know what you're talking about."

Her lips twisted and she jerked her head toward Delaney. "It's her, isn't it? You were with her in the hallway by the bathrooms a minute ago, wasn't it?" Lisa stepped back. "Thank you for the dance, but I'll find someone else more interested in *me*." She walked away like a model, strutting her stuff in her leopard stilettos and mini skirt.

Her exit left Tuck standing in the middle of the dance floor, looking like a fool. Heat rose up his neck into his cheeks and he made his way back to the bar to retrieve his beer.

Reaper laughed and slapped his back. "What did

you say to piss her off?"

"Nothing."

"Oh, come on, she didn't leave you high and dry for nothing."

"She didn't want to dance with me. Can you leave it at that?" Tuck tossed the last of his beer to the back of his throat, thinking it was time for him to leave.

"Man, you've got a bug up your butt tonight." Reaper grinned and took a swig from his mug, then nodded toward Delaney. "What do you think about me and O'Connell?"

Tuck choked, nearly spewing out the beer he'd been in the process of swallowing. "You and Del— O'Connell?"

"Yeah, why not?"

"Her call sign is Razor for a reason." Didn't he know it? She'd cut him off like an unwanted appendage. Tuck's pride still smarted from her brush off. Never mind he'd always been the one to leave the woman behind.

"She's not that cutthroat, just with men who get too fresh."

"What brought this on?" Tuck demanded. "I thought you two were just friends."

"Hell, we've known her for the past couple months. And since she's been hanging out with us, I've gotten to know her even better." A smile played on his lips. "I think she's a keeper."

"She's not a fish."

Reaper chuckled. "I know. What I'm getting at is that I think it's time to take it to the next step."

"Next step? Like dating?"

"No. I got to thinking. You and me, we're not getting any younger."

"So?"

"We never really know when our next mission will be our last."

"Don't be so fatalistic," Tuck grumbled and stared at his beer.

"It's true. We could be dead tomorrow, and what would we have to show for it? Who would give a rat's ass?"

"Your point?"

Reaper turned and held out a ring box. "I'm marrying that girl."

Chapter Three

Tuck schooled his face to show no emotion, while inside he reeled. "Don't you think a date should be the next step? Aren't you missing the important part about getting to know her?" he asked, when he wanted to shout, *No! She's mine!* Even though she'd just ended it with him.

"We're already close. All those nights we spent together, drinking beer, talking, watching football. We know what each other likes on our pizza."

"That's no reason to get married."

"She likes beer, she watches football, knows me, and finishes my sentences."

"Because you talk too slow."

Reaper stared across the dance floor at Delaney and went on as if Tuck hadn't spoken. "She's everything I ever wanted in a wife. Tough, smart, beautiful, and she can fly a helicopter like nobody's business. Man, she's got it all."

He had a lot of good points. Delaney was all those things and more. She liked pepperoni pizza and her favorite position was—ah hell. Tuck had to tell Reaper he was crazy to even consider asking her. She wasn't interested in him or getting married.

And if she were to marry anyone, the man would be him. *Damn it! She's taken!* he yelled inside. But the truth was, she was free to marry anyone she liked. Not that she would. She'd told him just as emphatically as he'd told her that she had no intention of ever getting married. "It's too soon. You barely know her. You haven't even kissed her." Tuck frowned. "Have you?"

Reaper grinned. "Not yet, but I can wait. And I want the first time to be special. The main thing is that I want to grab her up before someone else does."

"She's not the last cupcake at the party. And, Reaper, there's something you should know." He took a deep breath before continuing. He wasn't a man who'd kiss and tell, but staying silent while his buddy launched a campaign to woo the woman Tuck had slept with just wasn't right.

Before he could go on, Reaper responded. "I know she's not a cupcake, but I'm betting she's as sweet. You and I both know she's special."

Tuck stared at Delaney as she tripped over Big Bird's big feet and laughed to make him feel better about his clumsiness. "She's special, all right. And she's also t—"

Reaper wasn't listening. "We could ship out tomorrow and she would never know how I feel." He was in his own world, talking through his reasoning for rushing into something with Delaney. "I'm telling her I love her tonight."

"I wouldn't."

"Why? Don't tell me the confirmed bachelor is in love with her too?" Reaper laughed. "That'll be the day."

"No, Reaper, really, there's something you need to know about O'Connell." *And me.* What could he tell his friend? That he'd already staked a claim? He'd been with Delaney and she'd nixed any claim by telling him the liaison was over before it had barely started. No, Reaper fancied himself in love with Delaney, and he was willing to risk everything to make her his.

The song chose that moment to end, and Big Bird led Delaney back to the bar. She smiled and laughed, her gaze going to Tuck and then sliding to the woman in the leopard skirt sitting at the end of the bar. Delaney's brows rose, her mouth tightening.

Tuck clamped his mouth shut, refusing to show any emotion.

Delaney's eyes narrowed.

Reaper grabbed the box from Tuck and hopped down from his stool. "Tonight's the night."

Tuck snagged Reaper's arm and whispered, "Ask her on a date, tell her how you feel, but don't ask her to marry you until you know where she stands."

"I've made up my mind." Reaper stuffed the ring in his pocket and squared his shoulders. "Wish me luck."

Tuck ground his jaw. "Reaper, don't—"

Reaper strode toward Delaney, stopped directly in her path, and dropped to one knee.

Tuck started after Reaper, wondering how his friend had gotten this carried away in such a short time.

Looking from Reaper to Tuck, Delaney frowned, then her gaze swung back to the man on bended knee.

Tuck wanted to slap his palm to his forehead and would have, if it would do any good. Reaper was on his own mission and nothing would stop him.

Reaper held out the ring box and announced loud enough for all to hear, "Delaney O'Connell, I love you. Will you make me the happiest man in the world and marry me?"

Her cheeks bloomed with color and she bit her bottom lip. "Cory...I..." Wide-eyed, she glanced at Tuck for help. "I...good Lord, I barely know you."

Reaper smiled up at her with his gotta-love-this-surfer boy good looks and a pleading expression on his face. "I've known you long enough to know you're the one for me. Why waste time, when none of us know how long we have on this earth?"

"True." Delaney bit her bottom lip. "But—" She glanced again at Tuck with a *help me* look in her eyes.

Tuck moved toward the two as others gathered around, shouting and patting Reaper's back, waiting for Delaney's response. Not that she'd say yes, but even the chance that she could made Tuck's gut knot.

"Cory, I like you, and I think you'll make someone a great husband. But—"

He raised his hand. "Sweetheart, even if you don't say yes right now...please, don't say no until I have had the chance to prove to you I'm serious."

Delaney's cell phone rang, giving her the excuse she needed to avoid an immediate answer. She glanced down. "It's my CO. I have to take this."

Reaper nodded, waiting patiently, his smile in place, happy and ready to face a future with Delaney.

Delaney hit the talk button. "O'Connell." She listened, nodding though the speaker couldn't see her. At last, she spoke. "Yes, sir. Zero-five-thirty in the morning. I'll be there ready to punch out. You too, sir." She hit the end button and stared across at Tuck and then down at Reaper. "I'm moving out in the morning."

"What?" Reaper rose to his feet. "You can't leave. Not yet. You haven't answered my question. What about us?"

"It'll have to wait," she said. "Duty calls."

Reaper gathered Delaney's hands in his. "You can't leave me like this. I need to know."

With relief making his muscles a bit jittery, Tuck stepped up beside his friend. "Save the heartache, Reaper. She's not interested in a relationship."

Delaney's brows puckered, her gaze narrowing. She squeezed Cory's hands and smiled. "I'll tell you what, Cory, let me think about it. When I get back from deployment, if you still feel the same, I'll give you an answer. Right now, I need to go."

"Fair enough. " He jumped to his feet. "I can drop you at your townhouse."

"That's okay. I drove myself. You guys don't have to leave. Stay, have a drink for me. I'll let you know my answer when I see you again."

"Wait." He snagged her hand, stopping her from making a quick escape. With a gentle smile, he brushed the hair from her cheek. "Won't you at least give me a kiss goodbye?"

Irritation shot through Tuck. "Reaper, she's not—"

Delaney shot a stony glance at Tuck, leaned up on her toes, and brushed a kiss across Reaper's lips.

A cheer went up from the men standing around

them.

Tuck balled his fists, his back teeth grinding together as Delaney dodged past him without saying a word and ran from the club into the night. He stood for a moment wondering what had just happened. When it hit him, he groaned. His best friend had just asked the girl he'd slept with the night before to marry him. And she hadn't said no. Not only had she not declined the proposal, she'd kissed Reaper in front of their team.

What the fuck? Why didn't she tell him no? She'd told Tuck she wasn't interested in a long-term relationship. For most, his parents excluded, marriage meant a lifetime commitment. Until death and all that. "I gotta go," Tuck said.

"Now where are you going? The woman I love just ran out on me. I could use a designated driver to get me home safely."

Tuck grabbed Big Bird. "Make sure Reaper gets back to base all right, will ya?"

Big Bird draped a ham hock of an arm over Reaper's shoulders. "Yes, sir."

"Sober." Tuck jabbed a finger in Big Bird's solid wall of a muscular chest. "You're to drive sober."

"No shit, LT. I got this."

"I might as well leave," Reaper said. "Now that O'Connell's gone, I don't feel much like partying."

"Then stay to humor Big Bird. He's got to practice the two-step O'Connell taught him."

Reaper glared at Tuck. "I'm not dancin' with him."

"No, but you can find a girl that will. Use that

surfer boy charm of yours."

"I don't surf."

"You know that, and I know that, but they don't." He nodded toward the women seated in groups around the club. "When you tell these girls you're from San Diego, they'll be impressed and might take pity on Big Bird for you. Help out the poor guy. I'm out of here."

"Traitor." Reaper turned away. "Go on. You need your beauty sleep and Big Bird needs a girl. I'll get him one, then I'm right behind you."

Tuck walked to the exit and, once outside, sprinted to his truck. Too late to stop Delaney, because the taillights of her Jeep disappeared around the corner at the end of the block.

Traitor. The word resonated in Tuck's conscience. His *guilty* conscience. If he hadn't sat like a damned fool while Reaper talked about Delaney, the man might not have proposed, and Delaney wouldn't have kissed him.

The night was not supposed to end this way. By now, he and Delaney should have been burning up the sheets. Instead, Delaney would be packing to ship out, with an outstanding proposal on her mind from another man.

Damn. Delaney is shipping out.

He'd gotten used to having her around. More nights than not, they were together. Either at his apartment or hers. With her leaving in the morning, she'd be up packing into the early hours. He had to see her one more time. Apologize for not stopping Reaper and for letting him propose in front of their entire team. There was no good way to back out of what had happened. Reaper would lose face and take a boatload of razzing from the team. Tuck would look like a heel to his friends and the camaraderie would suffer if any of them found out he'd been sleeping with Delaney when his best buddy wanted to marry her.

First things first. He had to see Delaney before she shoved off.

He drove like a madman to beat her back to her place, parked in an alley, and jogged up to her building before she pulled into the parking lot.

Hooking her purse over her arm, she climbed out of her Jeep and turned to the staircase leading up to her apartment.

Tuck stepped out of the shadows.

Delaney jumped and stifled a scream that turned into a string of curses. "Goddamn SEALs. You're like snakes, lurking in the grass waiting to pounce." She stepped around him.

Tuck grabbed her arm and pulled her against him. "Snakes don't pounce."

"Okay, slither." She slapped his chest. "How could you let Cory go that far?"

"He didn't give me a chance to talk him out of the proposal."

"What am I supposed to do now?" She pulled free and stalked up the stairs, stopped, and glared back at him. "He asked me to marry him in front of your entire team."

"It wasn't all of them." Tuck followed at a safe pace. In her mood, she might push him down the flight of steps. And damned if he didn't deserve it. "You could have said no."

"What I hate is that I love Reaper," she said before turning toward her door.

"You what?" He took the steps between them two at a time and caught up with her as she shoved her key into the lock. "You love Reaper?" She'd never told him she loved *him,* much less *Reaper.*

"Of course I do." She rolled her eyes. "Like a brother."

"And me?" Tuck thumped his chest, anger burning a hole in it.

The starch melted out of her stance and she sighed. "You know how I feel about you."

No, he didn't. He smoothed a hair behind her ear, his hand drifting down the side of her neck, over her collarbone to trail across one breast. "Like a brother?"

"I'm not into incest." She sighed, caught his wrist, and held him there, her eyes closing as she pressed her breast into his palm. "Does that answer your question?" Her voice had gone all husky and sexy like when they were making love. Then her eyes opened and she stared, challenging him, sparks flying between them.

Tuck took her key from her, twisted it in the lock, shoved her through the door, and slammed it behind them with his foot. Then he tossed her over his shoulder and marched toward her bedroom.

"Put me down, Tuck. I'm not a sack of potatoes." She pounded his back with the flat of her palm.

He patted her fanny. "I know you're not a sack of potatoes. But this was the quickest way I knew to get you into bed." Once inside her bedroom, he tipped her over and tossed her onto the mattress.

She lay in the middle, skirt hiked up to her hips. "You could have tried asking."

Shit. Even her frown was sexy.

"What time did you say you're bugging out?" He yanked his shirt over his head and threw it against the wall.

Delaney licked her lips, her gaze raking over his naked chest. "Five thirty. I have to be at my unit, packed and ready to go."

His cock hardened in an instant. "How much time do you need to pack?"

"At least an hour."

With the barest of glances at the clock on her nightstand, Tuck ripped open his button fly and shucked his jeans. "It's midnight. That gives us four hours. Let's rock this boat."

Delaney's hand hesitated on the hem of her shirt. "What about Cory?"

Tuck grabbed her foot, and slipped the strap of her sandal off her heel, then flung it to the floor. "I'm not into ménages."

She pulled her shirt over her head, her breasts bobbing with her movements. "But he may still think I'll say yes."

"Will you?"

"He makes good husband material for a girl interested in that kind of commitment."

Tuck growled, advancing on her. "I seem to

recall you telling me you didn't care about commitment. In fact, you gave me the brush off on more than one occasion."

Her lips twisted, then slid upward in a smile. "I did, didn't I? And see how much good it did?"

He placed a hand on her leg, his fingers skimming up the insides of her thighs to the hem of her skirt. "Our relationship is purely physical."

"It won't last." Her breathing hitched as he skimmed his hand across her damp panties. "No...it...won't...laaast." She bit down on her lip, her knees parting to give him better access.

"With you leaving tomorrow, we don't have much time left in our short-term relationship."

She shook her head, her chest rising sharply on a gasp as he flicked her favorite spot again. "Then stop wasting time."

One last, teasing stroke, then Tuck ripped the zipper down on her skirt and tugged it over her hips and thighs and off her legs.

Delaney lay on the sheets in her underwear, biting her lower lip, her hand sliding into her panties. "God, I'm wet."

Those words made him want to rip off her panties and drive into her, hard and fast. A thin swatch of silk was all that stood between him and doing just that. But he wouldn't let their last night together be all about him. He wanted her to be just as turned on as he was at that moment. More so, if he did it right.

He couldn't believe he'd gotten this far with Delaney, and thanked his lucky stars he had.

When other members of his team had hit on her, she'd shut them down in a heartbeat, earning a reputation for being frigid and unapproachable by most. But when Delaney was alone with him, she was as wild in bed as she was in the cockpit of her Black Hawk. She knew exactly what to say and do to make him hard enough to drive nails with his dick. He lunged for the nightstand and the stash of protection she kept there.

"Losing it, frogman?" With her thumb, she hooked the elastic of her panties and slid them just far enough down until the soft curls of her mound peeked out. For a moment she held them there as if challenging him. Then she slipped off the panties and rolled onto her belly, her legs dangling over the side of the bed. "Three hours and fifty-eight minutes."

He fumbled the packet and dropped it on the floor. "Damn it, Del, you drive me insane."

She glanced over her shoulder, her brows hiking and a smile lifting the corners of her lips. "Insane with lust, I hope?"

"You know it." He ripped the retrieved package with his teeth, rolled the condom over his rock-hard erection and let go of the breath he'd been holding. "Let's shake this boat."

"Bring it." She arched her back, her damp entrance glistening in the light shining in from the other room.

Tuck grabbed her hips and positioned himself behind her, his member nudging her slick opening, then waited. "Promise me you'll come back." He didn't add what they both knew was on their minds.

Come back *alive*. Not in a box.

"Oh, please." She leaned back, trying to make their connection more intimate.

He pulled away. "Promise."

"I promise to do the best I can. But if you deploy, too, you have to make the same promise."

"I promise to do the best I can."

"Deal. Now are you fucking me, or should I start that packing I need to do? Three hours and fifty-five minutes, frogman."

He thrust into her, long and hard. Her channel clenched around him, dragging him deeper. Hands on her hips, he pumped in and out of her, smacking her buttocks for the loud clapping sound she so loved.

"Damn it, Tucker. Harder!" She rocked back, their combined motion forcing the bed to rock on its legs.

When he thought he was getting close, he slowed, bending over her back to cup her breasts, tweaking the nipples.

"Holy hell, Tuck, don't stop now."

"I want you with me." His hand slipped down to her sex, parting the folds to find the swollen little strip of her clit. He rubbed it, eased himself out, coated his finger in their juices, and slammed back into her, then slathered the moisture on the nubbin of her desire.

Her breath caught, her body tensed and her fingers curled into the comforter. "Now. I'm coming now." Her voice hitched as her body arched and her head tipped back.

Tuck gave her a moment to ride the first wave of

her orgasm. Then he backed out of her, scooted her up the bed, and climbed between her legs, sliding back in to take her. He wanted to see the way her green eyes darkened as she came apart.

Smooth, strong, athletic legs wrapped around Tuck's waist and Delaney dug her heels into his ass, forcing him as deep as he could get. The pressure erupted in an explosion of sensations that spread in waves outward from his cock to the tips of his extremities. He stayed buried inside of her, his dick throbbing his release. When he could draw in a new breath, he collapsed on the bed beside her, rolling her over to face him, maintaining the connection.

As they lay in each other's arms, Tuck stroked the swell of her breast, bringing the nipple to a hard little peak. He wanted to say it. The "L" word perched on the tip of his tongue. He bit down to keep from letting it slip out. Passion was one thing. Love was entirely different. What was it he felt for Delaney? He wasn't sure, but his own track record with that elusive emotion hadn't given him much hope of finding it. Still...Delaney had come the closest. "Del, you know how I feel about you, don't you?"

She sighed, snuggling her face against his chest. "Umm. You think I'm hot in bed, and that I'm a good helicopter pilot."

He snorted softly. "More than that."

Her eyes opened and stared up into his, a smile playing at her lips. "What more does a woman want?"

"What with Reaper asking you to marry him..."

After a long pause, she said, "I'm not getting married anytime soon."

"And I'm not a good candidate for the institution."

She leaned up on her elbow and stared downward. "Tuck, you can't judge yourself by your parents' lack of commitment."

"Yeah, and what's your excuse for avoiding tying the knot with some poor schmuck?"

Her eyes darkened. "I have my reasons."

Reasons she hadn't wanted to share. A jab of anger pinched his chest and he stiffened. He wanted to demand she tell him why she was against marriage. She knew his rationale. Why didn't she trust him with hers?

"I'm leaving tomorrow." Her hand smoothed across his chest. "Don't be mad now."

Delaney was right. He didn't want her to leave angry at him for pushing an issue that shouldn't be an issue at all. They weren't committing to each other, so why should he care if she didn't tell him her reasons for avoiding marriage? "Fair enough. Just know this. Despite my feelings on long-term commitment, I care. I don't want anything bad to happen to you."

"And accepting Cory's proposal would be bad?"

Tuck let out a sigh. "Reaper's a good man and he'd love you to his dying day. But he's not the man for you." He stroked his finger along her arm, letting it trail over the side of her breast. "You wouldn't be with me now if you thought you had a chance to make things work with Reaper, would you?"

"No." She dropped her gaze.

"Then why string him along?"

"You have a point. And you care." Her hand

slipped down his chest to his cock. "Why don't you show me how much you care, big guy?"

"Before I do, what are you going to tell Reaper?"

"Nothing until I get back from deployment."

"You'll let him suffer that long?"

"You didn't tell him about us." She gripped his cock and slid her hand to the base, relenting. "Maybe by the time I get back, he'll be in love with someone else."

Reaper did have a reputation for rushing into things before thinking about them. If Tuck hadn't been so immersed in keeping his relationship with Delaney a secret, he'd have seen it coming. "I should have made our relationship more public."

"No." She shook her head. "It's hard enough maintaining a tough-gal persona in front of my peers. Most of the men in my regiment resent me being there."

He'd been just as hesitant to let on that they'd been together. Problem was that he'd had such a deep distrust of women from a very young age. Delaney was the first woman he'd ever told about his crappy family life. Perhaps because the three of them had started out as friends, he hadn't wanted to reveal how far past friendship they'd progressed, afraid if he committed to their relationship, it would fall apart. Like his parents' had.

Delaney sighed, her hand rising to cup his face. "Look, I know you have issues with marriage and commitment. And it's understandable, given your family. But not all marriages end in divorce."

"You're saying my father, who's been married

three times, and my mother, going on her fifth husband, isn't normal?" He laughed without humor. "Why Cory would be idiot enough to propose is beyond me. Aren't there studies to prove more than fifty-percent of marriages end in divorce?"

"That gives people a fifty-fifty chance of it working." She shook her head. "Sometimes you have to take chances. Sometimes they pay off."

"Or get you killed."

Chapter Four

Delaney laid against the curve of Tuck's body, committing to memory the male, musky scent of their lovemaking, the feel of his hard muscles against her softer ones, and the way his breath warmed the back of her neck.

Four o'clock in the morning and she hadn't slept a wink, preferring to savor every last moment with Tuck. She hadn't packed, hadn't notified her landlord, hadn't done anything to prepare for her deployment.

She was headed to Afghanistan. Not that she was borrowing trouble, but she might not come back. As a member of the 160th Special Operations Aviation Regiment, she'd be flying into enemy territory to deposit and pick up the Special Operations forces, be they Army, Navy SEALs, or marines, on some of the most dangerous and highly classified missions imaginable. The chances of being shot down by the Taliban were high.

Meanwhile, her heart would be back in Virginia with Tuck.

She'd known from the start that Tuck had commitment issues given his family background plus he was a Navy SEAL first, anything else came second. Including her. But sometimes she dreamed of hearing him say those three words she'd longed to hear.

I love you.

Three of the most powerful words in the English

language dictionary, as far as Delaney was concerned. As she headed into the warzone, she'd have to content herself with the knowledge Tuck cared about her. Possibly loved her, but wasn't willing to admit it and jinx their bond.

Delaney had committed one of the ultimate mistakes she'd told herself she'd never do. Falling in love with a man in the military. Now it was too late. There was no going back. Her heart belonged to Tuck.

Cory and Tuck fell into formation on the pavement outside the Ops tent where their commander worked. Gunny called them to attention, then performed an about-face to hand off to Skipper, Commander Raymond Janek.

The man stood like a tree, six-feet, four inches of hard muscle. He stayed as fit as any of the younger SEALs standing before him, and demanded no less from his team than he did of himself.

Without preamble, Skipper announced, "We're headed to the sandbox. Report with your deployment bags here at Zero-five-thirty in the morning. That gives you exactly twenty-two hours to shit, shower, shave, and pack. I suggest you get to it. Am I clear?"

"Sir, yes, sir!" The team yelled in unison.

"Dismissed."

The team fell out and ran for their vehicles.

"Nothing like buggin' out on short notice," Cory said as he jogged alongside Tuck toward his vintage '67 Mustang. "It's probably just as well. I'd hate to be stuck here, coolin' my heels waiting for O'Connell to get back with her answer." He stopped beside his Mustang. "I don't know. I'm thinking she might say no." He shook his head. "You think she could love a man like me?"

"I know she loves you. Question is *like what?*"

"What do you mean like what?"

"Does she love you like a lover, a brother, or a friend?" Hell, Tuck knew, but why burst the guy's bubble now?

Cory's brows dove together. "What did she tell you?"

"I heard what you heard. She'll think about it." That still angered him. She could have come right out and said *no*.

Cory exhaled a long breath as he pulled out his keys and jammed them into the lock. "I hope that's a good thing. Means she wants to think about it. I hope by the time we get back from the desert, she'll say yes. As it is, I don't know if I can wait that long."

"Guess you'll have to."

"She give any clue as to where she's headed?"

"You know this stuff is classified." Tuck glanced at a spot over Cory's shoulder.

"Yeah. But I was hoping she'd trust us enough to tell us, or scuttlebutt would get back to someone on the team."

"I wouldn't ask. No sense puttin' her in the position."

"You're right. Guess you're the better man. I'd have asked, if she hadn't run out so fast. And she didn't answer her cell phone later. Lord knows I tried to call her ten times."

A wash of guilt tightened Tuck's chest. Her phone had been in the kitchen, the ringtone specific to Cory ringing several times.

They'd ignored it.

Tuck had a fifteen-minute drive to get back to his house. He made it in ten, grabbed the bag containing his deployment gear, extra uniforms, boots, undergarments, and toiletries that he kept stowed in his hall closet. After a quick look around, he left everything as is. The less anyone knew about his movements, the better. He didn't know where in the sandbox he was going or how long he'd be gone.

He hoped and prayed he'd be close to wherever Delaney had deployed. Only made sense for those who trained together to deploy together.

The call came in a week after she and her unit had boots on the ground at Camp Leatherneck. Her crew, consisting of her co-pilot and two door gunner crew chiefs, was called into the Tactical Operations Center, where TOP SECRET maps, photos, and intel lined the walls. Briefed on where they were headed and the number of people who'd be along for the ride, they were given the weather conditions, personnel movements, coordinates of their pick up and drop off, the number of men they would be carrying from the pickup point, and the amount of fuel they would be taking. The rest was on a need-to-know basis. Delaney was the Pilot in Command, or PC.

Delaney checked her flight bag for her HGU-56/P flight helmet, NVGs, maps marked with the roads and landmarks she could expect, and her electronic kneeboard, the Air Warrior EDM Tablet with data downloaded. She carried the memory card to be uploaded into the aircraft's radios and GPS. All data could easily be destroyed in the case of a crash, or if the aircraft was compromised. She threw in a bottle of water and stepped out of the ops center onto the flight line where her Black Hawk MH-60M stood. After a thorough inspection of the exterior and verification of the fuel levels, she climbed aboard, slipped on the helmet, downloaded the memory card, and began her checks on the interior controls.

Her copilot, Lieutenant K-9, settled in beside her and helped her complete the pre-flight inspection and checklist.

"Mac, Jones, ready?" Delaney spoke into her mic.

"Mac, ready," the senior of the two door gunners, Sergeant McKenzie, responded first.

"Jones, ready," Specialist Jones echoed.

Delaney fired up the rotors, and soon they were on their way to their first coordinate, a tiny patch of earth on the desert landscape in the southern province of Kandahar where she'd pick up six men and take them to the second coordinate. Enemy fire was possible at the first coordinate, and expected at the second.

Saving her adrenaline rush for the second leg of the journey, Delaney focused on the rendezvous with the team she'd transport.

The landing went without a hitch. The team, which appeared to be Navy SEALs, many of them bearded with scraggly hair, hopped aboard, wasting no time on the ground. Her heartbeat kicked up a notch, her thoughts, for a brief moment, bouncing back to Little Creek and Tuck. She wished he was there. After only a week, she missed him so much she physically hurt. Once the team was aboard, she took off, pulling her thoughts back in line with the mission at hand. She didn't have time to reminisce and couldn't afford to lose focus.

Dusk claimed the sun as it dipped behind the mountain range to the west. Darkness would settle over the desert before they arrived at the second coordinate. As they took off, the team lead stepped up behind her with a topographical map of the area. He'd switched his helmet for a headset and stuck out his hand. "Lt. Reed Tucker, US Navy SEAL."

Delaney's heart skipped several beats, and she schooled her face before turning to the man outfitted for battle. "I believe we've met."

"O'Connell?" Tuck's grin lit up his face. "What are you doing here?"

"I suppose the team that trains together plays together." She wanted to say a whole lot more, but refrained. "Who've you got with you?"

"Reaper, Big Bird, Fish, Dustman, and Gator." He shook his head. "I didn't know you'd be here, much less taking us out on this mission."

She stiffened. "Does it make a difference?"

His smile disappeared. "Not to me."

Delaney nodded. Some men had dumbass superstitions about females being part of a mission. They believed having a woman along would jinx them, spelling out trouble from the get-go.

As the only female pilot allowed on a trial basis into the 160th with the specific purpose of flying combat missions, Delaney wanted to be treated like any other male pilot. She was as good, if not better and she had to prove it, over and over, while proving she wasn't bad luck to a mission.

Tuck gave Delaney a brief rundown of her role in what was about to go down.

The team was infiltrating a small village reported to be harboring Amir Khan Muttaqi, one of the Taliban leaders the U.S. had been after since the war in Afghanistan had begun. They were to infiltrate, capture him, and get out before the Taliban knew what hit them. Small footprint, minimal casualties.

Delaney was to set them down on the other side of a hill from the village under cover of darkness. The men would move in, find and secure the target, then she'd fly in to retrieve them.

That would be the sticky part. Helicopters weren't known for their stealth abilities, and the distinctive sound of rotor blades beating the air alerted people on the ground before the helicopter came within firing range. Delaney understood the danger.

Tuck laid a hand on her shoulder. "You got this?"

Delaney knew he didn't doubt her ability to understand and perform the mission. His unspoken question was, could she handle it?

A flash of anger fueled her response. "Got it."

Tuck returned to his seat in the back.

"Let's do this." Delaney checked her controls,

fuel levels, and took off, swinging north toward the small village located in the hills. As darkness cloaked the desert, she switched to NVGs, flying at an altitude high enough not to be seen from the ground below, and out of range of Taliban-controlled rocket-propelled grenades or RPGs.

The mission proceeded like clockwork. Delaney hovered on the opposite side of the hill where the village was located. The men fast-roped to the ground and hustled toward the hill.

Delaney and her crew stayed long enough to provide cover, then flew south a couple clicks to a wide open, deserted location and landed to await word from the team.

Delaney sat behind the controls, wishing she could pull off her gloves and bite her nails. Waiting had never been her strong suit. The guys on the ground would see action before the night was over.

Question was, would they live to tell?

Tuck took point, and the rest of the team fanned out in a V to his sides and behind. Armed with M4A1 rifles with the SOPMOD upgrades including sound suppression and night vision devices, they moved through the darkness like cougars stalking prey.

Treading silently over the rocky terrain, Tuck eased to the top of the hill and checked for posted sentries. He spotted one twenty yards from where they hunkered low. He pointed to Reaper and motioned for him to take out the guard.

Reaper slipped away from the others and, within minutes, dispatched the man with the point of his knife. Quick, quiet, and efficient, Reaper rejoined the others before they descended the hill toward the village. Halfway down, Tuck held up his fist and the group of men stopped. He pointed to Reaper and Gator to join him.

Through his NVGs, Tuck picked out the bright green signature of a man standing guard on top of a building at the south end where the road led into the village. Tuck dispatched Gator to take him out. Not long afterward, Gator signaled from the top of the building, with one flash of a red lens light up at the hill.

The team moved into the village, Tuck counting mud-brick, fenced compounds until he reached the sixth one on the left, set back a little from the main dirt road. Inside the walls would be a house and storage buildings, all looking very similar, like mud boxes, either square or rectangular. Until they crossed over the fence made of large stones stacked, chinked, and covered in a mortar-like mud, they couldn't see into the structures.

Tuck was first to pull himself up over the wall and drop to the ground on the other side. Reaper was right behind him. Gator and Dustman brought up the rear while Big Bird and Fish remained on the other side of the fence, positioned at the far corners to watch for anyone attempting to go in or out. They'd provide back up, should the team need it.

Tuck pointed to Reaper and indicated he should sweep the left, while Tuck took the right and they rounded the main structure within the wall. No one stirred. Tuck stopped in front of the back door, tested the handle, then slid his knife into the gap, and pushed the lock open.

He slipped in and Reaper followed.

Once inside, they moved room to room, passing a living area and then a bedroom where three adult women crowded on a sleeping mat on the bare floor with small children tucked against them.

In the next room, the heat signature of a man lying on the floor caught Tuck's attention. He appeared to be an older man, not the Taliban leader they were supposed to find. Either he would be found in another building on the compound, or they had the wrong home.

Tuck motioned Reaper ahead of him and out of the home, pulling the door closed behind him.

Reaper moved on to the next building, similar in size to the first. Gator followed, the big guy so quiet, he was one giant shadow in the night.

Tuck joined them against the building. He directed Dustman to be the lookout at the corner, while Tuck, Gator, and Reaper stood beneath a window where they could hear the low hum of voices through a narrow opening.

Tuck made out some of the words in Pashto. They were talking about crops and the amount of money they could get for the current poppy harvest. When the man speaking mentioned how many weapons that would buy, Tuck's adrenaline shot up. This had to be the place. He nodded to Reaper and they ducked around the other side of the building to the entrance.

Tuck led the way, pushing against the door,

hinges squeaking slightly. He waited before entering, gauging whether or not the men in the back room had heard. When the Afghan's voice droned on, Tuck crossed the threshold and slipped past darkened rooms. Women and children slept inside some of them. He pulled doors closed and moved on, determined to make this extraction as quick and painless as possible. Where the hallway split at a T-junction, he sent Reaper to the right and he and Gator took the left, toward the sound of talking men.

As he reached the room, a scuffle at the end of the hallway behind him made him stop short, weapon at the ready. He shot a glance over his shoulder. A man had emerged from the room at the end of the hallway, adjusting his robes with one hand, carrying a gun in the other. When he spotted Reaper, he raised his weapon. Reaper swung the butt of his M4A1, catching the man on the chin so hard, a loud crack echoed against the dried mud walls. He slid to the floor.

A shout sounded from the men in the room in front of Tuck. Before the men inside made it to the door, Tuck dove through the opening, weapon ready.

Armed with AK47s, and handguns, five of the eight men in the room opened fire.

Tuck nailed two of the shooters.

Gator popped two others.

The last armed man flattened himself on the floor behind one of his dead buddies and fired wildly at Tuck and Gator.

One bullet hit Tuck in the chest, his flak vest protecting him, but the force of the bullet knocked him back against the wall. By the time he steadied himself, another round nicked his left shoulder. He dropped to the prone position, aimed, and shot the man between the eyes.

Two of the other men grabbed the weapons of their dead compatriots. Before they could pull the triggers, Tuck and Gator fired, dropping them where they stood, leaving the last man alive. He stood tall, his black beard and mustache shaggy, unkempt, his head swathed in a black turban. He spat on Tuck and cursed him in Pashto. The man looked like the one in the photos from his mission briefing. They'd found Muttaqi.

More shouting out in the hallway pushed Tuck to action. Their team didn't have time to waste before the entire village descended on this location. When Gator grabbed the man's arm, Muttaqi fought back.

Tuck hit the Amir in the temple with the butt of his weapon.

The man fell to his knees, then flat on his face.

Digging a zip-tie out of his pocket, Tuck secured the man's wrists behind his back.

Gator slapped duct tape over his mouth, then flung him over his shoulder in a fireman's carry.

Tuck emerged into the hallway to spot Reaper cornered by two men, a third man in the process of pulling the pin on a grenade.

He lobbed the grenade at Reaper and dove into a room.

Tuck couldn't get to him fast enough and watched in horror as Reaper grabbed the grenade and flung it into the room after the retreating man. With no time to spare, Reaper dropped to his belly and shaded his eyes.

Tuck and Gator only had time to fling their arms over their eyes.

The grenade exploded.

The force of the explosion knocked Tuck and Gator backward, Muttaqi's body landing on top of them, the concussion making Tuck's ears ring and his head spin. As he pushed his way out from beneath their prisoner and sat up, his vision blurred, then came back into focus and his heart skipped several beats.

The entire wall where Reaper had been standing had crumbled onto Reaper and the three Taliban members. Dust choked the air.

Tuck staggered to his feet, off balance, a sense of urgency hard to grapple with when he could barely stand. He grabbed Gator's hand and pulled the man to his feet. They teetered together until they could stand on their own.

Muttaqi groaned through the tape on his mouth, thankfully still alive for interrogation later.

Tuck helped Gator load the man over his shoulder and shoved him toward the exit.

Dustman met them at the door, took Gator's load, and ran to the back wall of the compound, shoving Muttaqi over the top.

With Muttaqi out of the compound, Tuck went back for Reaper.

Two Taliban members, still alive but bruised and bleeding, had converged on Reaper and were digging him out of the rubble, cursing, something about ripping him apart.

Tuck aimed at the one nearest to him. "Hey!"

The men dropped Reaper's arms and lunged for Tuck.

Two bullets ended any discussion, and Tuck raced to where Reaper stumbled to his feet.

"About time you got here." He pressed his hands to his ears. "Can't hear a damned thing."

Reaper's voice came to Tuck muffled and almost unintelligible, effects of the stun-grenade's explosion. Though temporary, the condition didn't make for clear-headed thinking when they needed it most.

With Reaper leaning heavily on him, Tuck ran from the building into the night.

Shouts sounded all over the village, and the popping of semi-automatic weapons indicated other Taliban members were closing in.

Tuck grabbed his handheld radio. "Razor, extraction point B. Now!"

Her answer came quickly, "Roger."

They had less than two minutes to get to their rendezvous point alive. At the west end of the village was a flat field where the locals grew poppies. Most likely the crop the Taliban had been counting on to fund the purchase of additional weapons.

Gator and Dustman, with Muttaqi dangling between them, followed Big Bird and Fish along the road between high walls.

Tuck brought up the rear, a bad feeling twisting in his gut. The walls were like canyons, trapping them in and funneling them through like mice in a maze. All it took was one enemy soldier with a machine gun to take out all six of them. Weapons aiming upward, the team ran through the streets as fast as they could, carrying the dead weight of an unconscious Muttaqi.

If Tuck had it his way, he'd shoot the murderous Taliban leader and get his team out before they became numbers on some congressman's tally of the cost of Operation Enduring Freedom and the Global War on Terrorism.

He prayed the village inhabitants didn't have an RPG anywhere nearby. Not with Delaney on her way to collect them.

The report of rifle fire had them slamming against the walls shadowed from the moonlight. Fish took a bullet to his leg, hit the ground, and rolled back to his feet.

Big Bird made Tuck proud when he locked in on the sniper on the rooftop and expended one bullet on the man. The Taliban soldier tipped over the edge and crashed to a heap in the street in front of them.

The sound of rotors beating the air pushed Tuck forward, yelling, "Move! Move! Move!"

The six men and their prisoner burst into the open and ran, stumbled, or limped toward the field of poppies.

Machine gun fire peppered the ground behind Tuck. He didn't slow or stop. The helicopter appeared overhead and the door gunners laid down suppression fire until all the men were on board with Muttaqi.

The last one in, Tuck barely had his foot on the skid when the helicopter rose into the air.

A parting shot pinged against the side of the

Black Hawk as it rose higher, headed back to Camp Leatherneck where they were to hand Muttaqi into the care of military intelligence officers for interrogation processing.

His ears still ringing, Tuck pressed the headset to his ear.

"Tuck?" Delaney asked.

"Yeah, Del, I'm here."

"Cory?"

"On board."

"The others?"

"All present and accounted for." Tuck's heart still beat like a snare drum at a rock concert.

"What the hell happened?"

"We can talk later."

Silence for a moment.

"Tuck?" Delaney's voice filled his head.

"I'm still here."

"I'm glad."

Chapter Five

Delaney's hands shook on the controls as she guided the helicopter to Camp Leatherneck, their final destination for the night.

An hour of waiting had taken its toll. Along with the co-pilot and her door gunners, Delaney had been on full alert, NVGs scanning for heat signatures of Taliban fighters while their bird was on the ground, a dangerous place to be if someone decided to attack.

When the call had come through to pick up the men at the alternate location just outside the village instead of on the other side of the hill, she'd jumped to the worst conclusion. They'd run into trouble, maybe gotten wounded. Or lost one of the team.

Delaney didn't hesitate to fly into hostile situations, but the worst part of her job was when she had to airlift out a dead or dying soldier, SEAL, or marine. Every life was important. The men fighting in this endless war had family waiting for them back home—a mother, father, grandmother, wife, children, lover—someone who would miss them if they didn't come home safely. And her responsibility was to get them out.

During the past few months training as part of a joint task force, she'd come to know so many of SEAL Team 10, specifically the squadron of men that included Tuck and Cory. She loved most of them like brothers. But Tuck...there was nothing brotherly about the way she felt about him.

He was strong, capable and—despite his upbringing—caring, loyal, and would do anything for those he loved. She'd fallen for him the first time he'd walked her to her car, after they'd been at DD's Corral too late. There'd been nothing sexual about how he'd seen to her safety. That he was incredibly sexy, and had shoulders so broad he filled doorways, had nothing to do with how quickly she'd fallen. Well, maybe a little. His deep voice, gentle hands, and the way he held her in his arms on the dance floor had sent her determination not to fall for a military man soaring out the window.

He was everything she could want in a man. His loyalty to his team, and especially to Cory, was commendable.

To a point. But that point had long since passed when Cory proposed. Now they were faced with dangerous missions. If she broke the news to Cory that she had been seeing Tuck for the past month and a half, how would he take it? Would it put a dent in the camaraderie between Tuck and Cory, or any other member of the team? They couldn't afford that. She couldn't be the bone of contention between the tightly knit group of men. Not when they needed to focus on the mission.

The radio had yanked her out of her musings, back to the present and the danger the team now faced. She'd fired up the engine and, as soon as she could, lifted off, skimming the top of the hill and dropping into the valley below, the rotor wash flattening the poppies in the field where she landed.

She'd held her breath, praying they'd all come out alive, counting as they emerged from the cover of the buildings. Not until the last one entered the helicopter and she was able to lift off did she release the breath she'd been holding.

She cared about all the men she transported into and out of battle. But having Tuck and Cory on board added to the burden, reminding her that not only did the people she carried have someone back home who loved them, she cared about them as well. She had a huge responsibility to herself and others—bring them home safe and alive.

Now that they were safely up in the air, the helicopter sweeping away from the village and gaining altitude, Tuck's pulse regulated. The flight to Camp Leatherneck went quickly. Working in the dark with a flashlight and first aid kit, the team performed self-aid buddy care on each other for those wounded in the explosion and subsequent firefight.

Fish would need to see a surgeon to retrieve the bullet from his leg. He hoped to be back with the team soon afterward. Nothing kept a good SEAL down for long.

Reaper sat in the middle, fiddling with something in his hands.

Tuck shone a light at him to discover he was turning the ring box he'd used to propose to Delaney. As SEALs they weren't supposed to bring anything personal to the battle, they didn't wear nametags or rank insignia. If caught, the enemy would use anything to torture information out of them. Why the hell would Reaper bring the damned ring?

The entire trip out to the sandbox, Tuck had tried to bring up the subject of Delaney and why proposing to her wasn't a good idea for Reaper. Each time, Reaper cut him off, insisting he knew what he was doing.

Short of telling Reaper he was seeing Delaney and that they were a thing, he didn't know what else to do. If word got out he was dating the 160th Black Hawk pilot responsible for transporting them on missions, he or Delaney could be shipped back stateside and reprimanded.

When the chopper landed at Camp Leatherneck, medics and intel officers were there to greet them. Fish argued about being carried out on a gurney, finally agreeing to let the army female medics drape his arms over their shoulders and help him limp to the waiting ambulance. Grinning, he looked back over his shoulder and winked.

The medics wanted Tuck to report to the hospital for sutures.

He refused, insisting the wound could be patched with a bandage. To prove the point, he unbuckled his Protech Tactical Armor Plate Carrier or PTAC, eased it over his shoulders, and dropped it to the ground. The absence of the weight made him feel immediately lighter and more agile. And naked.

With the cool desert night air blowing over his skin, his imagination carried him back to the bed he'd shared with Delaney a little more than a week ago, her smooth body pressed against his.

Reaper sat on the bumper of the ambulance

beside Tuck, another medic checking him over for concussion and lacerations from the grenade explosion. Reaper pushed the medic's hand away from his face. "Gunny's set up quarters for us. Let's go."

"Shouldn't you be at the hospital?" Tuck asked.

"The doc said I looked okay, no concussion."

"Then head for quarters. I'll be along in a minute. I need to debrief intel." Tuck really wanted to catch Delaney on her own, after everyone left. Images of stolen kisses bumped up his adrenaline and pulse.

The medic cleaned his wound and applied a sterile bandage, warning him to keep it clean or the gash would get infected.

When Reaper finally stood, he stretched and flexed his muscles.

About that time, Delaney climbed down from the helicopter and removed her helmet.

"I'll be damned." Reaper laughed. "Tuck, look who our pilot was."

"I know."

Reaper frowned. "You knew O'Connell was flying, and you didn't tell me?"

"I wanted everyone to focus on the mission, not the pilot."

Reaper ran a hand across his dusty, shaggy hair. "Think she's had enough time to decide?"

Panic tightened his throat. "Reaper, we're in a war zone. Now's not the time to push a girl to marry you."

"I can't think of a better time. Away from home, feeling lonely and afraid." He flexed his biceps. "Big, handsome SEAL to her rescue. It's a romance novel come true."

"Reaper, you really have to get a clue. She may not have agreed to marry you because she doesn't love you that way." How many times did he have to say that before Reaper got the hint?

"If that was the case, she would have said no when I asked her."

"You asked her in front of all of our friends. She's nice enough to save your ugly face from embarrassment."

Reaper hung back, his frown deepening. "I hate it when you make sense. What I hate worse is that she might have said no if I hadn't asked in front of our friends." His frown lightened. "If she's leaning toward saying no, maybe I need to show her I meant what I said. She probably thinks I'm not serious."

Tuck wanted to slap a palm to his forehead. He'd have to come right out and tell the guy Delaney wasn't into him. "Look, Reaper—"

Reaper wasn't listening. He raised his hand and yelled, "O'Connell!"

So much for seeing Delaney alone.

The medic had barely taped down the last edge of the bandage when Tuck jumped up, shrugged his shirt over his shoulder, and hurried after Reaper and Delaney.

"So I was thinking, how about you and me grab a bite of breakfast together in the chow hall?"

"Sounds like a good idea." Tuck fell in step on the other side of Delaney and winked at her. "But shouldn't you be heading to the hospital for that CAT scan?"

Reaper's brows dipped. "No, and I was asking O'Connell here to breakfast. Just the two of us."

"And five hundred of your closest friends? Come on, Reaper, you'd leave a brother behind?"

"When it comes to O'Connell?" He snorted. "Hell, yeah."

"I have a suggestion." Delaney stopped. "Why don't the two of you have breakfast, and I'll check in with my commander, get a shower, and hit my bunk."

"Are you assigned to Camp Leatherneck?" Cory asked, his face brightening.

"I am. But I want you both to know, I'm not fraternizing with either of you." She pointed to Reaper then to Tuck. "Got it?"

Tuck figured she was telling them both to keep their relationship on the down low. He nodded, grinning. Determined to play along. "Come on, Reaper. Let's see if the chow hall is open this late."

Reaper snagged Delaney's hand. "I meant what I said. I love you, O'Connell. And come hell or sandstorms, I mean to marry you some day."

"Cory, I—"

"I know." He raised his free hand to stop her. "You don't want to make a decision until we get back stateside, and you're probably thinkin' I'm a flirt and couldn't be satisfied with just one woman. But you're wrong. If that one woman is you, I know I'll be perfectly happy to give up the others."

She laughed. "So noble, Cory." Her voice dripped sarcasm.

He sighed. "Just don't say no or make up your

mind until I've had a chance to prove it to you."

"But I—"

"Please. Don't decide yet." He grinned, kissed her fingers.

Like a royal pain in the ass and let go. Tuck grimaced.

"Come on, Tuck. I'm starvin'."

Tuck cast a frowning glance back at Delaney.

She shrugged and turned the opposite way, most likely heading for her tent and a shower.

Being on the same post as Delaney had its challenges. When deployed, the situation was even more difficult. Though he and Delaney were equal rank, having sex or sexual relations while deployed was frowned upon.

His groin tightened. Tuck never backed down from a challenge, but if he was going to risk his career as a Navy SEAL, Delaney O'Connell was worth it. And SEALs were known for taking risks most men wouldn't dare.

Delaney stomped away from Tuck and Reaper, steaming as she went. Why the hell hadn't Tuck told Reaper about them? They'd had over a week in which he could have brought up the subject at any time.

She ground to a halt, her flight bag banging against her knees.

Unless Tuck wasn't ready to make the fact known to his closest friend that he was in a committed relationship. Which he wasn't and had made it clear he didn't want to commit. Ever.

Was he that gun-shy when it came down to

commitment? His parents had really screwed with his brain. For a big, tough, eats-bullets-for-breakfast SEAL, he was running scared of her and the fact they could be in love. He probably thought that, like every other person in his life, she'd leave him.

His mother had left him every time she'd found a new lover or husband. Worse, she'd left him with his father who'd been the harshest disciplinarian with no love left for the boy he'd help bring into the world.

Damn. She would have to break it to Cory that she loved him as a brother, and there was no way the feeling would grow into anything more. Hell, she'd tried. But he hadn't let her get a word in edgewise.

She continued on her way to the operations tent where she reported to the Officer In Charge, debriefed on the mission, and then gathered her flight bag and headed for her tent. Exhausted, in need of a shower and some time alone, she was disappointed to find her tent mate wide awake and in the mood to talk.

Captain Lindsay Swinson sat on her cot with her feet up, removing the polish from her toenails. The sharp scent of acetone permeated the tent.

Delaney wanted to grab her towel and clothes and make tracks for the shower tent, but she had to get past her red-haired roommate first. A friendly, outgoing woman, Lindsay loved to talk. She worked as a nurse at the medical clinic on Camp Leatherneck, and knew a lot about what was going on in the camp. The reason was because she wasn't shy about asking. And with her rich Georgia accent setting her victims at ease, they usually told her more than they ever intended. "Oh, Del. I'm glad you're back safe. How'd it go?"

Reluctant to talk about the mission, she shrugged off the strain of what had happened. "Everyone got back alive."

Lindsay glanced up, her open face serious for half a second. "That's wonderful."

A long pause followed, as if giving a silent prayer for those who had not been as fortunate.

Shaking nail polish remover onto a cotton ball, she asked, "Transport anyone yummy?"

"I don't normally taste my cargo, whether supplies or people." Oh, yes, she'd brought back one of the yummiest SEALs in the Navy.

Her tent mate bent to rub polish off yet another toenail. "Have you heard anything from your sweetie-pie back in the states?"

Delaney debated her answer. She could ignore Lindsay and pretend she hadn't heard. Or she could tell the woman her sweetie was there at Camp Leatherneck. Or she could just say, "I heard from him."

Lindsay sat up, her attention back on Delaney. "And?"

"He's doing okay."

"Okay? Without you?" Lindsay shook her head. "No man should be okay without his woman."

"I'm not his woman. We're just..." What were they?

"Lovers?" Lindsay's smile quirked. "Sweetie, you've had love written all over you since you got here. You miss him, don't you?"

Delaney couldn't lie. With her toiletries kit in hand, a robe, and shower shoes, she paused. Had she missed Tuck? *Oh, hell.* "Yeah, I guess I do."

"And is that a crime?"

"Could be." Delaney sat on the edge of her cot, shower forgotten. "I came into the Army determined to be a lifer. Stay at least twenty years. Longer, if they'd have me."

"So?" She held up a bottle of neon pink nail polish to the light. "What's stopping you?"

Delaney drew in a deep breath and let it out. "How do people do it? How do they let themselves fall in love when they're in the military? Maintaining a relationship in the civilian world is hard enough."

"Honey, if you love someone enough, you make it work."

"What if they're in different branches of service and just as determined to make their job a career?"

"Then they figure out ways to see each other." Lindsay uncapped the bottle and the potent smell of nail polish warred with the still-lingering acetone. "They make choices and they do what they have to do."

"If only it was that easy."

"Sweetie, the more determined they are to make it work, the more they'll love each other."

Delaney's shoulders sagged. "If they're both willing to work on it." And that was the rub.

"Oh." Lindsay bit her bottom lip. "Like it's more one-sided?"

"Yeah. What if one is in it for the long haul and the other isn't?"

Lindsay's brows rose. "Ah, that makes it different. Does the person who's thinking long haul know whether the other person is really against commitment?"

"She doesn't know." Delaney shrugged. "And then there's this other person who has declared his love and proposed."

"Is this third person sexy, nice, long-term material?"

"Yes."

"Does she love him?"

A lump formed in Delaney's throat. "Yes and no."

"Either it's a yes or a no. Can't be both."

"She loves him like a brother."

"And he's proposed." Lindsay tapped a naked fingernail to her chin. "Now, my mamma always said a bird in the hand with a ring is always a better choice than one in the bush without."

Delaney laughed. "Now, you're making that up."

The nurse gave her a lopsided grin. "Okay, but dad-gum, girl. A sexy guy proposes to her and she isn't saying yes, but she loves him."

"Like a brother," Delaney added. "And he's best friends with the other guy."

"Good grief, Delaney. How convoluted is this scenario?"

Her gut knotted. "As complicated as it gets. She didn't say no to the guy who proposed."

Her nail polish forgotten, Lindsay stared at Delaney. "And why the fool-darn-heck not?"

"He told her not to decide, but to think about it.

And he's such a good friend, she hates to break his heart."

The light in Lindsay's eyes danced. "Does loverboy know the boyfriend asked her to marry him?"

"Yes, and so does his entire unit. He did it in front of them."

"Sweet Jesus! Pass the eggs and grits, he had a set of balls on him to do that."

"Yes, and he would have lost face in front of them had she told him she wasn't interested in him, but in his best friend."

"And loverboy was there and didn't say anything? Didn't stake a claim or punch out his lights?"

"No." Again, that was the crux of the matter. Tuck hadn't told Cory that he'd been seeing her. Now Delaney had a lie by omission and a dangling proposal hanging over her like a broken rotor, ready to crack, fall, and decapitate anyone standing too close to the bird.

"Honey, you should have stuck to the truth from the get-go. Men don't appreciate a woman who keeps them hanging when there's clearly someone else in the background."

"I know. You're right." Delaney gathered her things and stood. "I'll tell her to fess up."

"You do that, honey. And let me know how the fellas take it."

Toiletries in hand, Delaney stepped through the tent door.

"Good luck, Delaney," Lindsay said with a gentle smile. "If she tells the truth, they'll understand."

"They might understand. But will they forgive?"

"If they love her, they'll do anything."

Her head shook. "I'm not so sure."

"Then raise the stakes. Tell loverboy you come with strings.: She pointed a finger at Delaney's chest. "Either he accepts you with those strings, or you go your separate ways."

Delaney frowned. "I didn't say it was me."

Lindsay winked. "Sweetie, you didn't have to."

As late as the hour was, she would do no good to go stumbling around camp searching for the two men in the dark. Whatever she had to say, she'd have to do in the light of day. With a purposeful stride, she reached the shower tent, took a quick shower to wash off the dust from the flight, and pulled on her robe.

When she emerged from the shower tent, wearing flip flops and carrying her boots and uniform, a shadow slipped up beside her.

Before she could throw her boots at the figure, he slipped an arm around her waist, crushing her back against his front and clamping a hand over her mouth.

"Shh. It's me, Tuck." He dropped his hand from her mouth and turned her to face him.

"Damn it, Tuck. You can't go around scaring a girl to death all the time."

"You were so deep in thought, I'd have startled you either way. At least, this way I got to hold you in my arms for a moment."

He wore a tank top, gym shorts, and tennis shoes.

"How'd you find me?"

"I pulled a few strings." He bent to sweep her lips with his. "Are you mad?"

"I don't want anyone getting the idea we're fraternizing."

He eased her into the deeper shadows between a tent and a Quonset hut made of sturdy metal. "How's this?"

She raised her arms, pressed her body into his, her damp towel, T-shirt and flight suit dangling down his back. "Better." All he had to do was part her robe and...

Tuck slid his hand up the back of her thigh and beneath the edge of her robe, cupping her naked bottom.

She'd gone to the shower with only her robe and what she'd been wearing, so flustered by her talk with Lindsay, she'd forgotten clean underwear and her pajamas.

Now she was glad she had.

Tuck lifted her, wrapping her legs around his middle, his cock nudging her entrance through the fabric of his shorts. "You make me hotter than a desert scorcher."

A thrill of excitement seared through her veins like a lit fuse racing toward dynamite. "Are you sure no one will see us?" The potential of getting caught added to the nerves and lust fluttering in her belly. Her breathing grew rapid, shallow, barely able to keep up with her lungs supplying the oxygen to her brain. All the blood in her body seemed to rush to her core—heating, slicking and sensitizing her to his every touch.

"Everyone is asleep, or manning their guard posts. We're alone here," he said.

"But we're in the open."

"Not behind this tent. No one comes through here."

"How do you know? You've been in this camp less than an hour."

"Long enough to find you." He reached between them, locating her warm, wet opening and sliding two rough fingers into her.

Oh, yeah, he'd found her all right. Delaney bit down hard on her bottom lip to keep from moaning. She arched her back, her robe falling open, giving his mouth access to her breasts.

He accepted the offering, sliding his tongue across a turgid peak, making the nipple harden to a tight little bud. Then he nipped, rolling the tip between his teeth, while pumping his fingers in and out of her.

"This is so wrong." She gasped.

"But it feels..."

"So right," she said, her words rushing out as his thumb slipped between her folds and stroked the nubbin of her desire.

He chuckled as he shifted his attention from one breast to the other. "I don't suppose you brought protection with you?"

"I always take a condom to the shower." She snorted.

"I'll take that as a no." He sighed. "I guess I'll have to wait, but that doesn't mean you have to." He grinned, kissed her lips, and settled her on her feet.

A rush of disappointment filled her, only to be brushed aside as he pressed her against the metal building, the darkness concealing them from prying eyes. With his knee, he nudged her legs apart, parted her robe, and trailed his hand from the curve of her neck downward, over her breast, past her ribs and lower, his lips following the path of his fingers, distributing feather-soft kisses and tempting nips along the way.

Delaney squirmed, wanting more. Wanting to tell him she wanted more, but biting hard on her tongue to keep from begging out loud. They couldn't be caught; being found could mean a court martial offense. At the very least, if caught, they'd receive an Article 15 and she might be grounded or sent back to the States. She might even jeopardize her position with the 160th Night Stalkers.

For a moment, the weight of the consequences threatened to overwhelm her and make her call him off.

Then he dropped to his knees, parted her folds, and tongued her, there.

All thoughts were propelled into the darkness as the feel of his mouth on her most sensitive parts sent her spiraling out of control, her heart beating like the rotors on a helicopter, faster and faster until she thought it might explode out of her chest.

Tuck slid his tongue into her channel and swirled it around, then returned to stroke her pleasure center until she dragged her nails across the metal building behind her, seeking purchase as her senses launched into the stratosphere. Her head spun and her muscles tensed like a tightly loaded spring. The tingling started at her core, shooting outward as her body jerked in spasms.

Still, Tuck didn't let up until she could take no more.

Delaney grabbed him by the ears and dragged him to his feet.

"Hey, easy there. I need those." He laughed, sliding his body up hers until he pressed her against the metal, warm from the day's desert heat. "Like that much?"

"Too much," she whispered as she dragged air into her starving lungs. "Want more."

"Sorry, baby. I didn't come packing." He cupped her cheek and brushed his mouth across hers, then dove in to take her tongue as aggressively as he'd taken her down there.

His mouth tasted of her musk. Delaney threaded her fingers through his short hair, pulling him closer. "I don't care. Take me. Here. Now." She ran her hands down his arms to where his shirt disappeared into the waist band of his shorts. Hooking her fingers in the elastic, she tugged the shorts over his hips, far enough for his cock to spring free.

"Uh uh." He shook his head. "It's too risky."

"Like what you just did to me wasn't?" She ran her leg up the back of his thigh and curled it over his hip then, bracing her hands on his shoulders, wrapped both legs around him. "Sure I can't change your mind?" Leaning her back against the building, she lowered herself down over him, taking his thick girth into her wetness, sliding down over him like a well-lubed glove.

"Baby, your argument is very convincing." He thrust into her, pinning her against the wall.

She raised herself up to the tip of his cock. "How so?"

"You cover the point implicitly." Again, he thrust into her—slow, hard, and filling.

Her breath rushed from her lungs and she had to refill them before she could speak again. "Are you not challenging my supposition?"

"You bet I am. I challenge you." He powered into her, slamming her back against the wall. "And raise you one." He rammed into her again. "No, two. Ah hell. You make me crazy." He hammered into her over and over, until he drove into her one last time, burying himself deep inside her. He held her hips so tightly his fingers dug into her flesh. His member throbbed against her channel and he held his breath, his jaw rock hard.

Then he pulled free, loosened her legs from around his waist, and turned to the side as he ejaculated, his hand easing his straining cock.

A smile slid across Delaney's face, a surge of power making her chest swell. "Turn you on much, frogman?"

"Too much." He eased his member back into his shorts and turned. "I wish we could go somewhere for the night."

Delaney shrugged. "I have a roommate."

"I'd take you back to my place." Tuck ran a hand through his hair. "But I'm sharing a tent with Cory."

"About Cory..." She sighed. "He won't let me tell

him no."

"You can't marry him." He tucked a loose strand of hair behind her ear. "Not after what just happened."

"Cory thinks he loves me." Delaney leaned her cheek into his palm.

Tuck pulled away his hand, his eyes narrowing. "Love doesn't last."

Disappointment tugged at Delaney, even though she'd known how Tuck felt about long-term commitment. "It did for my parents. They loved each other from the time they started dating in high school until the day they died."

"They were the exception."

The warmth of their lovemaking slipped away with the cool desert breeze. Delaney pulled her robe tighter around her body and stepped out of the shadows. "So, you don't think it could happen for you?" *And me?* She wanted to add, but bit down on her tongue, afraid if she said it, he'd run the other way as fast as he could. Not that Tuck was a coward when faced by enemy gunfire. But commitment was a four-letter word to him. Any sign of it and he ran the other direction.

He was already shaking his head. "Look, Delaney, I like you and all..."

Her disappoint blossomed into a slow-burning anger. "I feel a *but* coming."

"I told you from the beginning, I'm not into commitment."

"What are you afraid of?" Delaney tapped a finger against his chest. "Afraid you might find some happiness? Cory isn't afraid to go after what he wants."

He grabbed her finger and held it, his grip punishing, hurting her hand. "Cory isn't right for you."

Chilled in the moonlight, Delaney tugged her hand, trying to break Tuck's hold. "You're hurting me." *In more than one way.*

He finally let go. Tuck moved, and the full light of the moon shone down on his face, exposing the hard lines and a muscle twitching in his jaw. He looked like he wanted to say something, but he clamped his lips tight and stood as still as the stone his heart was carved from.

Delaney wanted him to say something, wanted him to rant and rave and tell her she couldn't marry Cory. Not because he wasn't right for her, but because he loved her himself. But snow would fall in the desert before Tuck admitted to loving anyone.

"Face it, Tuck, you're not in a position to tell me who is right or wrong for me." She backed away from him. "Do me a favor and leave me alone." She spun and marched away, thankfully before the tears slipped from her eyes. She hurried to her quarters, hoping, but not betting, that he would follow her and declare his love. *Ha!*

She stumbled back to her tent, tears streaming down her face, ashamed that she cried at all. Kicking herself for loving a man who couldn't love her back.

Tonight, she'd allow herself to cry.

Tomorrow, she'd move on.

Chapter Six

Tuck paced outside his tent until the sun pushed up over the desert landscape to the east. No matter how he went over the conversation he'd had with Delaney, the ending didn't come out any better. As always, he drove away the women he met. Purposely, and with no regrets, for the most part.

Until Delaney.

Most of the women he'd pushed out of his life had been civilians, clueless about the life he led as a SEAL. All they saw were his taut muscles and sharp uniform. They never understood why he worked out, why he remained in top physical condition, or the pressures of running an operation. They would never know what killing someone felt like or understand the aftermath of losing a buddy in combat. That hollow, aching feeling and the constant instant-replay going on a SEAL's mind analyzing what went wrong, what he could have done differently that would have saved his fallen comrade's life.

Delaney would. She was as close to the action as she could get without being boots on the ground. As a member of the 160th Night Stalkers, she flew into areas most pilots would be afraid to fly. Being shot at was part of the job description. She'd accepted the danger along with the responsibility and honor of being a part of the squadron.

She was a good pilot, a strong woman, and so

beautiful she made Tuck ache. Then why the hell had he pushed her away?

Because she wanted what he couldn't give. Commitment. She'd never asked for it, but he could see it in her face.

Damn Reaper for exposing the elephant in the room. The one thing he'd always shied away from. Now, if he didn't come to terms with his deep-seated aversion to long-term relationships, he'd lose Delaney. Possibly to his best friend.

The man foremost in his thoughts emerged from the tent, shirtless, wearing his PT shorts and tennis shoes. "Hey, you up for a morning run before the temp gets too hot?"

Exhausted from a sleepless night, but too wound up to rest, Tuck grunted. "Yeah. Might as well." He pulled his tank over his head, and tossed it into the tent. "Let's go."

They set off, heading for the perimeter of the compound, remaining inside the wire where running was relatively safe without fear of tripping an improvised explosive device (IED). For the first lap, they ran in silence.

Then, breaking silence, Reaper said, "I've been thinking about how I can show O'Connell I'm serious."

Tuck's heart and feet missed a beat and he stumbled, righting himself immediately. After several more paces, he responded. "Are you sure she's the right one for you?"

"Never more sure in my life. She's special."

Unfortunately, Tuck couldn't argue with that. She

was and he knew it. Then why the hell couldn't he tell Reaper to back off, that, Delaney was his?

Reaper shot a glance his way. "You think she's holding back because she's got someone else in mind?"

"You'd have to ask her." Tuck gritted his teeth.

"Not that I'm afraid of a little competition. I know there are plenty of men for her to choose from, and she's hot enough to have her pick of the litter."

"She's not choosing puppies." Tuck wished Reaper would stop talking about Delaney. "Hell, she might not be in the market to choose anyone. Seems to me, she's pretty career-minded. Didn't she say she plans on being a lifer?"

"That doesn't mean she can't have a relationship, get married, and have kids."

"Flying for the 160th kinda precludes that, doesn't it?"

"The kids part for the time being, but not necessarily the rest."

"You two are in different branches of service. You'll never get stationed in the same place."

"I can live with a long-distance relationship. We won't be in the military forever." His arms chugged at his side. "And when we do retire, we'll have the rest of our lives to spend together."

"You both have no less than ten years left on your commitment, right?"

"Right." Reaper frowned at Tuck. "So?"

"That's ten years of seeing each other on weekends, if you're stationed anywhere near the other's base, or once a month if you're not."

"If a couple loves each other enough, they can make it happen. I'd be willing to make the commute as often as possible. O'Connell is worth it."

Tuck thought about what Reaper said. Right now, he'd move heaven and earth to be with Delaney as often as possible. But would that longing last? For ten years or more?

None of his parents' many marriages had lasted ten years. Five, tops. And they were together every day. What were the chances he could keep a marriage alive that long, if he dared to make the same foolish mistake as his parents and get married to begin with?

"Hey, isn't that O'Connell ahead?" Reaper's words knocked Tuck back into the here and now.

His pulse sped up at the sight of Delaney in her short, black shorts and gray army T-shirt, jogging ahead of them.

"No time like the present to start my campaign to win her heart." Reaper picked up the pace to catch up to Delaney.

His gut churning with anxiety, Tuck sped up as well.

"Uh, Tuck." Reaper slowed and shot a sideways glance. "You're crampin' my style, dude."

Tuck nodded and slowed, giving Reaper the lead, when he really wanted to trip him and take it himself. Without telling Reaper why he didn't want him to catch up to Delaney, Tuck had no reason to be angry with his friend. But he was.

Angry, tense and...jealous.

Fuck.

Reaper caught up to Delaney and fell in step

84

beside her.

Tuck slowed, jogging at a distance far enough away he couldn't hear their conversation, but close enough to hear Delaney's laughter. His chest tightened and before long, he had a hard time regulating his breathing. Finally, he slowed, turned, and ran in the opposite direction. He'd jog in the heat of the day rather than watch Reaper woo his girl. Instead, he ran sprints near the volleyball nets until he couldn't stand it a moment longer. After a while, he walked back toward his quarters, the long way. The path that would take him back by Delaney's tent. When he realized what he was doing, he almost turned around and headed back for more sprints.

Until he saw Delaney step out of the shower tent wearing clean shorts, a T-shirt and carrying her robe, towel, and toiletries in hand. That robe was the clincher.

Tuck's groin tightened on sight at how beautiful she'd been wearing it last night in the moonlight. And how naked, soft, warm, and wet she'd been beneath.

He sped up, determined to catch her. What he'd say when he did, he didn't know. Tuck only knew he had to say something. This deal with Reaper was eating at him and somehow the reaction had to stop.

Before he reached her, Reaper jumped out from another path, carrying a giant teddy bear with a big red bow tied around its neck.

Delaney ground to a halt and laughed.

At the sound, Tuck's gut knotted. Even her laugh was sexy. Damn.

She accepted the teddy bear, hugging it close and

burying her nose in the soft fake fur.

Where in hell had Reaper gotten a teddy bear in the desert?

Wherever he'd acquired it, Delaney was enjoying it more than Tuck liked. She leaned around the bear in her arms, lips puckered, aiming for Reaper's cheek.

Reaper turned at the last second and her kiss landed square on his lips. The asshole grinned, captured Delaney's cheeks between his palms, and kissed her again. "I knew you'd taste that sweet. And that's just the beginning."

Tuck's fists balled and he lunged forward. Before he'd taken two steps, Delaney shook her head. "Cory, I don't—"

"Don't decide anything." Reaper pressed a finger to her lips. "I'm not done yet. Be watching."

Reaper left before Delaney could complete her sentence.

Damn. Surely she'd been about to tell him to take a hike. After kissing her like that, she should have slapped him.

Unless...

Tuck stopped still in his tracks. Was it possible she could fall for Reaper?

After last night?

Delaney stared down at the bear. "What am I going to do with you?" She turned toward her tent, her gaze finding Tuck standing like a lunk in the middle of the path.

Her smile immediately turned down at the corners. She marched toward the tent, passing him with barely a glance. "What are you doing here,

Tuck?"

"You kissed him."

"So?" She stopped in the doorway.

"Why did you let him kiss you again?"

"Why does it matter to you?" She hugged the bear closer, like a shield between them.

Tuck wanted to rip the damned bear from her arms and tear it to shreds. "You don't love him."

"I could *learn* to love him. At least, he cares enough about me to share his feelings."

"Is that what you want?" He gripped her arms, the fuzz of the bear's fake fur burning against his skin. "You want me to share my feelings? I'll share. I'm pissed as hell."

"I don't see why?"

"You know damn well why."

"I know that you aren't into commitment. I know from your track record that you've pushed away every woman you've ever let closer than a one-night stand."

"I didn't care about them."

"And you care about me?"

His grip tightened for a second then he loosened his fingers. "Yes."

"Enough to say three simple words?"

"What words?"

"Oh, forget it. We have nothing left to say. I'm done." Shrugging away from his grasp, she ducked into her tent and closed the door behind her.

"We're not done until I say we're done," Tuck practically shouted, making the group of soldiers in uniform passing by at that moment turn and stare.

"What are you looking at?"

"Man, you need to turn down the volume. Some people are still asleep," a staff sergeant said.

Tuck wanted to tell the staff sergeant to shove it, but thought better of that declaration. He outranked the guy and therefore had to set the example. And he wasn't doing a good job of it. Which made him even madder.

When the soldiers had disappeared around the corner, Tuck lowered his voice and said, loud enough for Delaney to hear, "Delaney, be reasonable. Come out and talk to me."

A red-haired woman wearing a sand-colored T-shirt and her army combat uniform pants poked her head out the tent door. "Captain O'Connell asked me to tell you to get lost. Hey, don't shoot the messenger." She raised her hands and shot a glance over her shoulder, then whispered. "But she's kinda mad, and talking will do you little good. Try later. And if that doesn't work, I'm off duty at seven tonight." She grinned and ducked back into the tent.

Wanting to rip the canvas off the structure, Tuck bit down on his tongue to keep from shouting his frustration, performed a tight about-face, and marched back to the tent he shared with Reaper. Damn right he'd be back later. Despite Delaney's declaration, the relationship wasn't over until it was over.

"Oh my, sweetie, he was mad." Lindsay dropped onto her bunk, a smile spreading across her face. "He's the SEAL you were talking about last night?"

Delaney set the teddy bear on the bed and replied through tight lips, "Yes. Perhaps the most aggravating man on the face of the planet."

"And the sexiest. Wow." She fanned herself.

The movement made Delaney's anger spike even more. "Don't get too excited. The man doesn't have a heart."

"No heart?" Lindsay's eyes widened. "Who cares? With a body like that, who needs a heart?" She reached for her boots and slipped a socked foot into the left one.

"I do." Delaney stared down at the stuffed animal.

"Did he give you the bear?"

"No, that was from his best friend."

"Oh." Lindsay clamped her lips closed for a second, then opened them again. "The one who proposed? I take it mister macho saw the whole thing and wasn't too happy."

Delaney nodded, the tension knotting her shoulders. She rolled her neck. "He has no right to be mad. If he didn't want Cory to go after me, all he has to do is tell Cory I'm his girl."

"But he won't."

"No."

"And you want him to."

"Yes." Delaney slumped onto her cot. "I want it so much, it hurts."

"I'm sorry."

"Me too." Her lips twisted as she stared across the narrow aisle between their cots. "You didn't sign on to hear my whining about men. I'll stop dumping my troubles on you."

"Honey, I've been eating sand for six months. Your love life is a breath of fresh air and helps to break the monotony. Dump away." She shoved her foot into the other boot and pulled the laces tight. "Unfortunately, I'm on duty in fifteen and I want to stop by the mess tent for a bite on the way. Save it all for me when I get off tonight. That is, if you're not working. Do be careful, if you are. I like having a roommate."

Delaney hugged the woman. "Thanks. I appreciate your patience and the shoulder to cry on."

"Anytime. Just stay out of my workspace."

Delaney frowned.

Lindsay smiled. "In other words, don't get injured or sick. I love seeing you, but not for those reasons." She stepped through the door, calling back over her shoulder, "See you later."

Left alone, Delaney dressed in her flight suit and boots and headed for her helicopter to talk with the maintenance crew. She wanted to do a complete check on the systems and assess any damage incurred when the bullets had been flying the night before. Arriving at night, she hadn't gotten a good look at the craft. She hoped the work would take her mind off her personal problems long enough to calm down. She'd need to get some sleep. The missions she flew were invariably at night and she'd need to be at her sharpest. Military matters trumped matters of the heart any day.

Or so she told herself.

Tuck returned to his tent, steaming hotter than the desert sun at midday.

Reaper was doing sit-ups, his feet hooked beneath the legs of his cot. "Have a good run?"

"Hell no." He bit out. Reaper had left a wadded T-shirt on the floor between the two cots. "Can't you pick up after yourself?"

Reaper crunched a few more sit-ups and stopped. He rose, retrieved the shirt, and stuffed it into his dirty laundry bag hanging from a tent pole. "What bug crawled up your ass?"

"Who said I had a bug up my ass?" Tuck ached for a fight. He needed to put his fist through something. And right at that moment, Reaper was the closest to him and the source of most of his anger. All he needed was an excuse and he'd land a fist in his roommate's face.

"Well, if you're not mad about something, you're mad at someone. Let me guess. Is it the commander? Did he ask you to clean the head?"

"I'm not mad at the commander."

"Then who are you mad at? I'm not into twenty questions right now. I have to get to the mess tent before O'Connell. I want to leave a candy bar for the cook to give her as a special treat."

"That's it." He rounded on Reaper, his fists clenched. "That's the reason I'm so jacked up."

"Because of a candy bar?" Reaper stared at him. "I have another if you want it."

"No, I don't want your goddamn candy bar. I want you to leave Delaney alone."

Reaper's brows dipped toward the bridge of his

nose. "O'Connell? Why? Did the commander find out I was courting her?"

"No. The commander doesn't know anything. But I do, and I want you to stop seeing Delaney."

"Why?"

God, could he do this? Tuck shoved a hand through his hair and turned away. "Just because I asked you to."

"Sorry, Tuck. That answer isn't good enough."

Tuck struggled for one that made more sense when his own thoughts weren't clear to himself. "You're not the right man for her."

"I'm not?" Reaper grabbed his arm and jerked him around. "Are you saying I'm not good enough for her? Just because I didn't grow up with a silver spoon in my mouth doesn't make me inferior. I'm a good SEAL, I make a decent living, and I care about her more than I've cared about anyone else in my life."

"That's not enough."

"Why?" Reaper crossed his arms. "Give me one good reason why."

"Because..." Heat built in Tuck's neck, rising up into his cheeks. He felt like his head might explode. "Just because, damn it! You're not right for her."

"And what made you qualified to be the judge?"

"You've never been serious about a woman before. You flirt with every female you come into contact with."

"I'm done with flirting. O'Connell is the only one for me."

"How do you know? Another woman could come along and off you'd go, panting after her.

Where would that leave Delaney?"

"I'm not going after another woman. I only want her."

"What if she doesn't want you?" Tuck gritted his teeth, ready to tell Reaper the truth. But something made him stop and hold his tongue. She'd pretty much ended it with him.

"I told you. I'm out to convince her. Either you're with me on it, or..." With a shoulder block, Reaper shoved Tuck. "Stay the fuck out of my way."

Chapter Seven

Delaney had actually managed to catch a few hours of sleep during the hottest part of the day. The heat helped to drain her of energy, and she'd lain down on top of her sleeping bag, wearing nothing but her shorts and T-shirt.

She was jerked out of a sweaty dream of making love with Tuck when an unfamiliar voice called from outside her tent.

"Captain O'Connell."

"Just a minute." She sat up and pushed her hair off her damp forehead, then got to her feet and staggered to the door.

A private first class stood at attention outside. "Ma'am, your presence is required in the ops tent."

"Thank you, PFC Olinger. I'll be there in five minutes."

The PFC saluted, executed a sharp right-face, and marched toward the ops tent.

The sun was well on its way toward the horizon, although the heat of the day still lingered. At least, the wind had died down and the sand had settled. Flying nights was easier than battling the buffeting winds and sandstorms of the daylight hours.

Delaney poured water on a washcloth and performed a spit bath, wiping away the sweat of the day before pulling on her flight suit and zipping it up the middle. Boots came next, and she checked her flight bag before stepping through the door.

Lindsay almost bumped into her. "Shoot. I was hoping for an update before you headed out."

"Nothing to update. I gotta go."

"The hot SEAL didn't come by and declare his undying love?"

"Seriously?" Delaney laughed, the sound lacking any humor. "Not gonna happen."

"You'd be surprised. If the other SEAL keeps up his courtship, his actions might make SEAL number one realize he can't live without you."

"I doubt it. In the meantime, I have to go." Delaney hurried toward the ops tent, anxious to hear the briefing on their next mission, hoping it wouldn't include the team of SEALs from the night before.

As she stepped into the operations tent, her hopes were dashed. The same SEAL team she'd transported the night before was there, Tuck and Cory watching her every move as she entered and took a seat. The room was crowded with another SEAL team, her helicopter crew and a second one, as well as the team of operations planners including the Afghan informant who'd been instrumental in the interrogation of the Taliban member they'd extracted the night before.

Lieutenant Colonel Cooley, the Army Special Forces ops planner, and Navy Commander Backus stood at the front of the tent near the computer screen depicting the tactical map of the area of operation.

Through an interpreter, the Afghan operative told them of a Taliban stronghold in a village in the mountains. An important meeting would take place that night to discuss an attack on NATO forces.

When the Afghan finished, he was excused from the room. Once he was gone, Lt Colonel Cooley and Commander Backus took turns briefing the plan of attack.

The SEAL team was to get in, take out the Taliban leadership, and get out as quickly as possible. The village was said to be heavily guarded by the Taliban so they'd have to come in under the cover of darkness. Two helicopters would transport the teams as close to the location as possible, drop them, and get away until called to retrieve the men.

Delaney sat forward on her seat, adrenaline already thrumming through her veins. The flight would be dangerous, possibly more dangerous than the night before. There weren't as many hills around the village to disguise their arrival and shield them from anti-aircraft weapons.

"An unmanned aerial vehicle will be deployed with the team. The weapons aboard the UAV will be used to take out the main target. But you must get a definitive target location. You know the drill, limit civilian casualties."

The SEAL team was given specific coordinates and departed to gather their weapons and gear, and do any last-minute planning amongst themselves. They'd have the toughest mission. Going door-to-door in a village was as dangerous as an operation comes. They never knew when the enemy would pop out of a building or a sniper would pick them off from above.

Cory and Tuck were the last SEALs out the door, both glancing back over their shoulders.

Delaney tried not to notice, refusing to look directly at them, though they were perfectly visible in her peripheral vision.

Lt. Colonel Cooley handed an electronic kneeboard and memory card to Captain Kuntz and the same items to Delaney. "Just remember, if the enemy is in range...so are you." He winked. "You two good to go?"

"Yes, sir!" Kuntz responded.

"I got this, sir," she replied, feeling more confident by the minute.

Fear wasn't a factor of the mission. If she let in fear, she'd put the rest of the team and crew in danger. Pilots of the 160th had to act, not think. They had to be ready to rush into dangerous situations without hesitation. They'd trained these kinds of missions over and over while back at Little Creek with the SEALs. She could fly this type of mission practically blindfolded. The only variance was live enemy fire. Minor detail.

"Let's do this." Delaney said.

By the time she stepped out of the tent, the sun had dropped below the horizon and the gray haze of dusk cloaked the desert. One by one the stars came out, twinkling in the sky above. Delaney loved flying at night. At times, she felt like she was a spaceship pilot, surrounded by the vastness of the universe.

Her father had instilled in her a love of the heavens and the curiosity that made her want to explore. She'd spent one childhood summer at Space

Camp in Alabama. With the space program winding down, she'd joined the Army and trained to fly helicopters. Not as high as space, but equally thrilling.

For a few moments, she stared up at the stars, wishing her father could see her now. Maybe he could. Heaven was only a heartbeat away. Delaney hefted her flight bag and headed for the helicopters to perform her preflight check. Her crew stood beside the craft, ready for her inspection. She went over each member's Air Warrior equipment, including the vest with body armor and armor plate, CSEL combat survival radio, NVGs, and knife. She and her copilot had been issued M9 pistols and ammo. In the cockpit, the crew stashed water and snacks.

Once she'd completed her crew inspection, her copilot checked over her personal equipment, then they began the aircraft preflight checklist. By the time she'd finished the exterior of the craft, climbed into the pilot seat, and strapped on the safety harness, the SEALs showed up, loaded for bear and appearing so dangerous, they could scare the locals into submission before they even lifted a weapon.

Decked out in the battle uniforms, PTAC and helmets, they all looked alike in the darkening sky.

Good. At least then she wouldn't know who she had on board. Each man equally important as the next. So what if Tuck got on the other aircraft? At least then she wouldn't be distracted by his presence.

The SEALs split into two details and climbed aboard the waiting aircraft.

Delaney started the blades spinning.

A hand on her shoulder was followed by, "Alpha

Team, five souls aboard."

"Roger," she responded, her heart leaping into her throat. She could almost feel the heat of Tuck's hand through the survival vest. Warmth and calm settled over her. Despite her resolve to remain unaffected by which team was aboard her aircraft, she was glad it was Tuck's.

At exactly the designated hour, Delaney lifted off the ground and swung north.

Following the route specified on her kneeboard and in the flight computer, Delaney kept a vigilant eye on the terrain below, employing her NVGs to pick out any heat signatures along the way.

By the time they reached the drop zone, all the stars shone bright in the sky. At least the moon wasn't adding to the brilliance of the night. Too much light and Al-Qaida manning anti-aircraft guns would be able to pick them off all too easily.

The two helicopters flew nap of the earth, hugging the terrain to avoid early detection. When they reached the drop zone, Delaney brought the Black Hawk to a halt, hovering twenty feet above the dry desert just outside the village.

Two by two, the men fast-roped to the ground, loaded with weapons and NVGs.

When her door gunner's voice came through her headset, "Drop complete," Delaney took off, heading toward the designated safe area where she'd await the call from the men on the ground. A wait that would be the longest thirty minutes of her life.

Tuck hit the ground first and ran for the village,

confident his men were right behind him. They'd practiced this maneuver so many times they performed as a well-oiled machine. Nearing the outer walls of the village, they encountered enemy fire.

Tuck gave the signal to drop in place. The other team followed the lead and hit the dirt.

After two more tracer rounds, Reaper had his man in his sights and picked him off with one shot.

Another hand signal and the team was on the move again.

Shouts went up from inside the mud and stone walls. The alert had gone out, and the people inside would be scrambling for weapons and positions.

Tuck and his team approached the east wall. When he arrived there, he bent down and the man behind him planted a boot in his back, leaped up to the top of the wall, and rolled to the other side so quickly no one could get a bead on him and fire before he was already over.

The next man flew over the wall, and the next until the fourth man topped the wall and reached down to grab Tuck's hand, hauling him over the top as he slid down the other side.

Once inside the perimeter, Tuck led the way again, moving down the narrow streets between the buildings and outer walls of each dwelling, counting the doors to the ones identified by the Afghan translator who'd gotten the information from the captured Taliban leader. As they neared the identified door, Bravo Team would be converging on the opposite side to head off any escapees out the back.

Gunfire erupted from above. A Taliban soldier

manning a machine gun fired down on Alpha team.

Each man hugged the wall, preventing the gunner on the top from getting a clear shot. All he could do was lay down suppression fire to keep them from stepping out to take a shot at him.

The gunfire came to an abrupt halt and they could hear the clinking of metal on metal. Most likely, the weapon had jammed.

Tuck motioned for Reaper to take the sniper, and he gave the signal for the rest of the team to follow him.

Behind Tuck, one round was fired, marked by a soft grunt followed by silence from the gunner. Reaper was a gifted marksman, an asset to any assault team.

Tuck moved on to the back side of the next compound and around the corner from his team. Reaper positioned himself at the corner, weapon ready, scanning the rooftops for more sentries.

With his back to the alley and feeling exposed, Tuck pulled C4 plastic explosives from his pocket. Despite their earlier argument, Tuck knew he could trust Reaper with his life. His friend had his back.

With quick, practiced moves, Tuck smashed the plastic explosives against the middle of the wall closest to the living quarters inside the compound. He pressed a detonator into the plastics and motioned Reaper back around the corner.

He pushed his guilt about his rift with Reaper to the back of his mind and concentrated on what would happen next as he checked his watch, and waited for the time agreed upon for Bravo Team to move into position. At exactly the minute designated, he held his hands over his ears and pressed the hand-held detonator. A small explosion shook the wall he leaned on. Another explosion sounded from the other side of the compound a couple seconds later, like an echo of the first.

Without waiting, Tuck ran around the corner and dove through the gaping hole in the wall. The tap, tap, tapping of gunfire kept Tuck low to the ground, bullets kicking up dust near his feet. He ducked and rolled into the shadows, pulled his NVGs in place, and scanned the corners of the building and the rooftop for the sniper. A moment later, he found him as he leaned around the corner to fire off rounds at the hole in the wall, then retreated behind the corner.

Tuck aimed, waited for him to appear again, and fired. The gunman grunted and slumped to the ground.

Reaper, Big Bird, and Gator entered through the hole and spread out. Fish remained outside the wall. He'd provide protective fire on their rear.

If they timed their moves right, they'd converge on the building at the same moment. Satellite photos had shown them where the entrances were. Bravo Team would take the main entrance and provide a distraction while Tuck's team blasted through the wall with more explosives and entered through the rear.

Everything was going as expected. Like clockwork. A niggling doubt insinuated itself into Tuck's mind as he pressed more C4 into the back wall of the residence. Enough to blow a hole without causing too much injury to the occupants inside.

Charges set, he held his ears and detonated. The wall crumbled, dust spewing outward. He motioned for his team to move in. No gunfire erupted from inside.

If the meeting was being held in this building, the attendees would have come B.Y.O.G. Bring your own gun.

Tuck didn't like it. Something wasn't right.

Before Tuck could alter the plan, Reaper was first in, as they'd planned in the drills they'd conducted at Little Creek back in the states. He rolled to the side, pointing his weapon at the empty interior. Tuck followed behind him, moving more slowly, peering through the dust-clouded interior of an empty room with nothing but broken furniture and rags littering the floor.

While Reaper moved toward the door leading to the interior, Tuck hung back. On the wall, someone had spray painted a message on the stucco walls in Pashto. Tuck took a moment to translate and when he did, lead sank to the bottom of his belly. He spun toward Reaper. "Reaper, don't go—" Tuck saw the trip wire just as Reaper bumped into it.

One minute, Reaper was standing in front of him, the next he was thrown across the room, along with half the wall.

Tuck flew back on his ass and the ceiling above him crumbled, caving in on top of him and Reaper. His ears ringing, Tuck forced himself to his knees and threw his body over Reaper as the stones and timbers crashed down, pummeling his back and head.

Something large and heavy hit the base of his

skull, knocking his helmet loose. For a moment, the world around him faded into darkness. He fought to shake it off. Reaper lay beneath him, having taken the brunt of the explosion. His body armor would have protected his torso to an extent and he still wore his helmet, but what about his face and limbs?

Tuck pushed against Reaper, the pressure on his back giving way a little at a time. Not fast enough.

Shots rang out beyond the building's walls. Big Bird shouted, Gator and Fish responded, but the sounds all came to Tuck as if from down a long, muffled tunnel.

He pushed again and a heavy beam rolled off his back onto the floor beside him, along with crumbled bricks and stone. Fumbling for his flashlight, he found it, switched it on, and shone it in Reaper's face. His eyes were closed, skin coated in dust.

Tuck pressed his fingers to Reaper's throat and prayed. When he felt the slow thump, thump of a pulse, he let go of the breath he'd been holding, and tapped Reaper's face. "Hey, buddy. Wake up."

Reaper didn't budge.

Bracing his hand on the ground, Tuck tried to stand. His leg was pinned by another beam. He twisted around and shoved the debris to the side before wiggling his foot. It hurt, but he thought he could stand. The main thing was to get Reaper out and back to the helicopter.

A mortar exploded close by, sending out a spray of more debris, the explosion reverberating in Tuck's already numb ears. If they wanted to get out alive, he had to move, now. The whole situation stunk of setup.

"Tuck?" Big Bird leaned into the building. "Tuck?"

"I'm here."

"You okay?"

"Yeah. But Reaper's down."

"Alive?"

"For now."

"We're taking rounds and mortars. Team Bravo was hit hard. Two dead, the other three heading back to the LZ."

"Fish and Gator?" Tuck asked, afraid of the answer.

"Injured but mobile. Need help getting out Reaper?"

"I'm not sure what injuries he sustained." Tuck pushed against the ground in an attempt to stand. Where he planted his hand was warm and wet. "Holy shit. Shine your light over here."

Big Bird stepped over the debris and focused his light on the ground at Tuck's feet. "Fuck."

Tuck ripped off his belt and looped it around what was left of Reaper's right arm, pulling it tight to stop the relentless flow of blood from his severed artery.

"We gotta get him out of here."

"I know. You go ahead of me. I'm right behind you."

"Tuck." Reaper's eyes blinked open.

"Yeah, buddy."

"Get out of here."

"Not without you."

"If I die, take care of Delaney for me, will ya?"

Tuck's throat closed up and his eyes stung. Whether from all the dust or the knowledge his friend might not make it out alive, he didn't have time to debate.

Reaper tried to lift his right arm, gave up, and caught Tuck with the left. "Promise."

Tuck ground his teeth together, adrenaline coursing through him. "Bullshit on all this talk about dying. You're making it out of here alive, so hang on." He bent, grabbed Reaper's uninjured arm, and dragged him over his shoulder in a fireman's carry. His ankle hurt like hell, but the injury was nothing compared to what Reaper had suffered.

His teammate grunted and then went completely limp, a deadweight hanging over Tuck, unable to balance or help to steady Tuck's load. Well, damn it, he didn't need help. He'd get him out if it was the last thing he did.

Stumbling over the stones, bricks and debris, Tuck made it outside the building where Big Bird was firing into the night.

"Go!" Big Bird yelled. "I called for transport. They're on their way."

Tuck ran through the alley, back the way they'd come, followed by the reassuring sound of Big Bird's weapon firing behind him. Gator and Fish were pinned at a corner, ducking around to fire in bursts.

As Tuck neared, they left the corner and charged past the intersection of two narrow streets.

Bullets pinged off the sides of the mud-covered compound walls. Tuck kept running. He had to get to the helicopter. If they could make the chopper, Reaper had half a chance to live. "Hang on," he said to his friend, again and again, like a mantra to cling to, getting him through the next few minutes.

Rushing past the last building and out into the open field, Tuck felt something hit the front of his leg, like a sharp sting. He ignored it and ran on.

The familiar whopping sound of helicopter rotors gave him hope for Reaper. "Please hurry."

"Tuck, wait!" Big Bird ran to catch up to him, grabbed his arm, and forced him to stop, pulling him to his knees. "Get down!"

Machine gun and rifle fire filled the night and the sky over their heads.

Tuck laid Reaper down, then covered his friend's body with his own.

A Black Hawk swooped in, guns firing at the fields ahead of them.

It was then that Tuck saw the silhouettes of men moving their way, carrying weapons. One of them stopped and lifted an RPG to his shoulder.

"No." Tuck couldn't leave Reaper to take out the Taliban man soon enough to stop the round from being fired. All he could do was watch in horror.

The round hit the helicopter above them. It jerked, then exploded in a ball of flaming aviation fuel, rotor blades flying loose, doors, skids and the fuselage breaking apart, flung across the sky like a broken toy.

Tuck's heart stopped in that second and he ducked his head, praying it wasn't Delaney's helicopter. "Dear God," he said. "Dear God."

The bulk of the craft crashed to the earth, the flames reaching toward the sky. The second helicopter flew in—low, fast, and deadly—firing everything it had at the men on the other side of the field.

When the machine guns attached to its belly ran out of bullets, the helicopter launched the rockets, the pilot expending every last bit of ammo. Then the craft turned back toward the town and landed near to the spot where Team Alpha had taken cover.

Team Bravo emerged from the walls of the village, two men flanking two others helping a third between them.

Tuck rose, and with Big Bird's help, carried Reaper to the waiting helicopter. With the door gunners providing suppression fire, the teams made it to the Black Hawk. Tuck and Big Bird laid Reaper on the floor. The others piled into the craft around him, hanging onto whatever they could find.

Tuck turned to Fish, the team corpsman. "Take care of him." Then he ducked back out of the chopper, followed by Big Bird, Gator, and two of Team Bravo's men. They scoured the area around the downed helicopter, careful not to provide a target for the Taliban. They found one of the door gunners lying among the poppies, the others appeared to have burned in the fire. Big Bird and Tuck carried the dead door gunner back to the waiting helicopter and loaded him next to Reaper.

"Let's go!" One of the door gunners yelled.

The helicopter, near its maximum load capacity, lurched from the ground and into the air.

Tuck bent over Reaper and shined his flashlight into his teammate's face.

He was deathly pale, all the color seeming to have leached out of his lips and he wasn't moving at all.

"Is he...?"

Fish shook his head and spoke loud enough to be heard over the rotors. "He's hanging on, but he's lost a lot of blood. You did good by applying the tourniquet when you did, or he would have bled out."

Out of the path of danger, without bullets flying past him, Tuck had time for the entire event to process. The building had been empty and set with a trip wire. If he hadn't stopped to read the writing on the wall, he'd have been the first one through the door. He would be the one lying there with his arm dangling uselessly, the muscles ground into hamburger meat.

He glanced at the back of the pilot's head. He couldn't reach her with the crowd of men aboard. Instead, he reached out to touch a door gunner's arm. "Who's flying this bird?"

The gunner's mouth was set in a grim line. "Captain..." The craft dipped and the gunner lurched, braced his hand on the inside wall and righted himself.

Tuck held his breath and waited for the man to finish, his heart in his throat, his stomach a massive knot.

"O'Connell," he finished. "Razor."

The air left his lungs in a whoosh and he slumped over Reaper. They'd lost an entire helicopter crew tonight. If they didn't get Reaper to a surgeon quickly...

Bullshit. They weren't losing Reaper, too. Tuck helped Fish stabilize the wounded arm, check Reaper 's other injuries, and establish an I.V. of fluids to replace some of what he'd lost.

Then Tuck prayed to God to spare his friend.

Chapter Eight

Delaney's hands were steady on the controls as she'd fired on the enemy. She couldn't think about the burning ruins of the other helicopter. The SEALs' lives depended on her keeping a cool head. One thing at a time. Kill the enemy, then get the men back to safety.

"Take that, you sons of a bitches," she muttered, the aircraft shuddering with the force of the machine gunfire and rockets launching.

"We got it from here," Mac, her senior gunner said, after she'd unloaded the last of the ammunition into the Taliban.

Without hesitating, Delaney turned the craft toward the village.

A group of men rose from the field and waved at her. She landed and tried to count but couldn't see from her side of the cockpit. "How many?"

"Four on their feet. They're carrying one."

Her throat constricted and she held onto the stick so tightly her knuckles turned white. "The other team?"

"Coming now from the village. I count four and they're helping another between them."

"All on board," Mac said.

Delaney wanted to take off before they encountered any more enemy fire.

"Wait," Mac said, before she could power up for

takeoff. "They're going back to check for survivors from the other helicopter."

The chances of anyone surviving an RPG direct hit were slim to none.

With her aircraft on the ground, she was a target and everyone inside was in danger. She counted the seconds until the team returned carrying a body.

As soon as Mac gave the go-ahead, she was up in the air and headed south. When they'd climbed high enough and out of range of the village, she asked, "What do we have?" What she'd wanted to ask was who was injured.

"One with a bullet in his leg. Another with a penetrating trauma, possible amputation."

Her fingers tightened on the controls. "Who is it?" she asked, praying it wasn't Tuck.

"Don't know. They all look the same." The gunner shouted, "Who is it?"

A moment later, he said, "Reaper."

Relief washed over her, followed immediately by guilt. "Will he make it?"

A hesitation before the answer came. "He looks bad. Real bad."

Delaney flew the helicopter as fast as it would go. She radioed ahead that they were coming in with severe combat injuries.

When she set down at Camp Leatherneck, medical staff converged on the aircraft. Delaney dropped down out of the cockpit and ran to the gurney where they loaded Cory. His uniform was shredded, his right arm swathed in bandages, shorter than his left arm.

Delaney gulped, fighting back ready tears.

Tuck stood on the other side of the gurney, far enough away the medics and corpsmen could do their jobs.

Cory's eyes opened and he stared up at her. "O'Connell?" He reached out with his good hand.

Delaney grasped his hand. "Yeah, Cory, I'm here."

"You never answered." He coughed, blood dribbling from the side of his mouth. "You gonna marry...me?" His eyes closed and Delaney thought he'd passed out. But then they opened and he looked at her, hopeful.

"Sure, Cory. I'll marry you. Just hurry up and get better," she said, tears spilling down her cheeks.

Cory closed his eyes, a smile pulling at his bruised and bloody lips. "Tuck?"

"I'm here," Tuck said, his voice raspy as gravel.

"Take care of her."

"I will. Until you're back on your feet. Because, you will be back on your feet."

"That an order?" Cory asked, his voice fading.

"You bet."

"Aye, aye." Cory's body went limp and the medics wheeled him into a waiting ambulance.

"I'm going with him." Delaney started after the medics.

Mac stopped her. "Ma'am, he'll be in surgery before you can get to the hospital. Likely, he'll be in surgery for a few hours. You might as well get through debriefing before you head that way."

Delaney stopped, torn between duty and her

heart. Cory was a dear friend and he was about to face one of the most traumatic events of his life. Losing a limb. He needed all the love and support he could get.

The ambulances drove away with Cory and the other SEAL who'd taken a bullet to his thigh. Mac left her standing on the tarmac. With the gurney gone with Cory and the others clearing the area, nothing stood between Delaney and Tuck. Nothing but a promise that changed everything.

She'd agreed to marry a man who might not make it through the night. And if he did, he had a long road ahead of him coming to grips with the loss of a limb.

Tuck loosened the strap beneath his chin and removed his helmet. His uniform was peppered with tears and blood. A large smear stained his chest and shoulder. He stared down at it and tried to brush it away.

"Yours?" Delaney asked through a tight throat.

He shook his head. "No, Reaper's." Then he looked up and stared across at her, the anguish in his eyes more than Delaney could bear.

She went and wrapped her arms around him. Her tears fell faster, soaking into the dried blood on his tattered uniform.

"It should have been me," he said, his voice harsh. He didn't raise his arms to wrap around her.

"You can't second guess what happened." Delaney swallowed hard on the lump in her throat. "It won't change the outcome."

"Reaper was one of the best." His body stayed stiff, rock hard and unrelenting.

"And he still is." Delaney leaned back, gripping Tuck's arms and shaking him. "He's not gone yet."

"You saw him." He glared at her, his lips peeling back in a snarl. "How can anyone live through that?"

With the image of Cory's ravaged arm seared into her mind forever, Delaney couldn't let it rule her life and thoughts. She straightened, pushing back her shoulders. Cory was her friend as well as Tuck's. He was too young to die. "We have lots of beer and pizza ahead of us. I can't drink and eat it all on my own." She laughed, the sound choked off by an escaping sob. "He'll make it."

Tuck looked to the sky and sighed. "God, I hope so."

"And when he does, he'll need all the support we can give him."

His gaze returned to her. "You promised to marry him."

"He needed to hear that." She chewed on her lower lip. "I couldn't say no."

"You do realize, you can't take back that promise."

She nodded. "I know." Cory's injuries were so severe, any emotional setback could kill him. For better or worse, she'd promised to marry Cory. And a promise was a promise. Even if she didn't love him that way, maybe she could learn to.

A medic stepped up to Tuck and pointed at his leg. "Sir, you're bleeding."

Delaney stared down at Tuck's pant leg, for the first time noticing the blood stain running from mid-calf to his ankle. "Damn, Tuck. You've been injured."

He shrugged. "Just a flesh wound."

"If you'll come with me, sir, I'll check it out." The medic hooked Tuck's arm. "You might need to see a surgeon."

Tuck shook off the hand, standing tall. "I'm fine."

"If it's all the same to you, sir, I'm just doing my job." The medic wasn't taking no for an answer.

"Go with the medic," Delaney urged. "The Navy needs you."

He paused, his gaze capturing hers. "And you don't?" he asked softly.

Her lips twisted in a wry grin. "I seem to recall the situation was the other way around."

Tuck nodded. "Doesn't matter anymore. Reaper needs you more."

Though she didn't want to, Delaney agreed. Still, it would have been great if Tuck owned up to loving her. Then again, an admission like that would only make their lives harder when she married Cory, knowing Tuck had changed his mind and wanted a long-term relationship with her. No, she was better off this way. There never was anything permanent between her and Tuck, which left her open to marrying a man she loved like a brother. If he lived to their wedding day.

"Captain O'Connell." Delaney's CO, Lt. Colonel Cooley, appeared beside her and gripped her arm. "Glad to see you're okay."

She stared up at him, fighting the tears. Members of the 160th Night Stalkers were the elite fighting force. They didn't cry.

Her commander shook his head and pulled her into a hug. "It's okay. Every pilot is allowed to express their grief. You wouldn't be human if you didn't."

She let a few tears trickle down her cheeks, then pushed back from the lieutenant colonel, wiping at the tears. "I had breakfast with Captain Kuntz this morning. He's got a baby on the way. His daughter starts kindergarten this year." She shook her head and swiped at more tears. "Sergeant Ryerson was one class short of his online degree, and Pickard was supposed to be best man in his sister's wedding next year."

"They'll be missed." The CO's jaw tightened and he stood for a few moments, gathering himself before he went on. "A retrieval team is on its way to recover them and bring them home."

More tears welled in Delaney's eyes as she pictured the funerals, the flag-draped coffins, and the wives and children of those lost. "Sir, my fiancé was the man severely injured in the explosion. I request permission to accompany him back to the States." She bit down on her bottom lip to keep it from shaking before adding, "If he lives."

"I'll see what I can do." He tipped his head toward the hospital. "Now, go. When he regains consciousness, he'll want to see a familiar face."

"Thank you, sir." Delaney hurried toward the hospital, pushing aside thoughts of the men who'd died, her hastily made decision to accept Cory's proposal, and the look on Tuck's face of resigned acceptance. Everything about loving a SEAL reminded her of why she shouldn't. Men who volunteered for such dangerous missions set themselves up for death or dismemberment. They were fearless adrenaline junkies. Women who married them waited in constant fear of getting that call, or of the chaplain stopping by with word of their soldier or SEAL's demise. She'd been through it once, when Max died on a mission.

If Cory lost his arm, he would never be deployed as a SEAL again. Most likely, he'd be medically retired or given a desk job. He'd be safe from going back in the line of fire. He would be the ideal husband for Delaney. She could love him without worrying about him getting killed. The idea didn't make her feel any better. Her heart couldn't switch gears so quickly, not when she still had feelings for Tuck, feelings that were more potent than the love of a brother.

Damn it. All the time she'd been holding back and telling Tuck they couldn't be together, she'd done exactly what she'd sworn she never would do. She'd fallen in love with a SEAL.

Again. Her realization didn't matter. What happened now wasn't about her or Tuck, or why they couldn't be together. Her focus was all about getting Cory through the night. Beyond that, she didn't dare think or plan.

Tuck refused to see the medic, heading straight for Commander Backus. The operation had gone south and he suspected the reason was more than coincidence. They'd been set up. The trip wire and the writing on the wall said it all. If Reaper hadn't stumbled on it when he did, both teams might have

118

been caught in the explosion. As it was, Reaper was the main casualty in the operation. The damage could have been much worse. Not that Reaper's life and health were any less important, but his sacrifice had saved the lives of the other men on the team. Cory was, unwittingly, a hero.

"You look like shit." Commander Backus greeted him with a handshake. "Glad you all made it back alive. I understand the op wasn't good."

"We need to check out the Afghani informant. I suspect he was part of this whole scam."

The commander's jaw tightened. "Can't."

"Can't? Why?"

"He's missing."

"So it was a set up."

"The man we captured last night hung himself right after the teams left in the helicopter."

"Fuck. Why didn't we get recalled?"

"We didn't discover our dead captive until after the shit hit the fan. By then, it was too late." Backus's glance raked over Tuck. "I want you to report to the hospital."

"I'm fine."

"That's an order."

"Sir, all I need is a shower. Reaper—"

"Is going to pull through."

Tuck clenched his jaw. "Sir, his arm."

"I heard." The commander's lips pressed together. "The docs will do their best to save it."

Tuck shook his head, knowing there wasn't anything anyone could do to save what was left of Reaper's arm. "Sir, that should have been me."

"What?" Backus stepped back, drawing himself up to his full height of six feet four inches, an inch taller than Tuck and every bit as intimidating a man as any SEAL could wish to be. "Did you tell him to trip over that wire?"

"No, sir, but—"

"We didn't sign on to be SEALs to wallow in self-pity or self-blame. Reaper won't, I guarantee it. And I don't expect you to, either."

Tuck opened his mouth to argue his point, but one look at his commander's face and he snapped his jaw shut. Backus was right. They didn't have room for second-guessing. What was done was done. No amount of regret would bring back Reaper's arm.

"Reaper is a SEAL. Whatever he has to deal with, he'll make it. We only train the best of the best." Backus led Tuck to the door and opened it. "I'll walk with you."

"Sir, I can make it on my own."

"And I don't give a rat's ass if you can or not. I'm checking on Reaper." Backus jerked his head. "Now, move."

Commander Backus knew exactly what to say to snap Tuck out of his funk. He walked tall, despite the pain in his ankle, just now flaring up as the adrenaline subsided. And the stinging bite he'd felt in the field outside that village probably was a bullet lodged in his leg. No matter the pain, he refused to show any sign of it. His injuries were minor. He'd keep all his limbs and live to fight another day.

The way he saw it, Reaper's days as a Navy SEAL were over. Tuck couldn't imagine what his life would be like if he couldn't be a SEAL. They were the family he'd never had. His brothers. He was closer to these men than he was to his father and mother, or his half-brothers from his mother's second and third marriages.

SEAL Team 10 was everything to him. Until Delaney had come along, he couldn't picture himself with anyone he loved more.

The woman in his thoughts waited outside the hospital tent, pacing.

Backus and Tuck stopped in front of her.

"Captain O'Connell." The navy commander held out a hand and Delaney took it. "I'm sorry to hear about the loss of Captain Kuntz, Lieutenant Metzger, Sergeants Ketchum and DeSpain. The recovery team is on its way back with their remains."

"Thank you, Sir." She let go of his hand and rubbed her arms as if she were cold. "At least, the families will have some closure."

"Any news on Reaper?" Tuck asked, looking for his answer in her expression.

Delaney glanced at the commander, refusing to meet Tucks' gaze. "A nurse came out a few minutes ago. She expects them to be with him for at least an hour. As soon as they stabilize him, they're sending him back to Landstuhl."

"Some of the best surgeons in the world are stationed there," Commander Backus said. "He'll be in good hands."

Nodding, Delaney continued. "They've got a critical care air transport team and a C-17 on standby, waiting for him in Bagram."

The news hit Tuck with a complex sense of relief and sadness. He and Reaper had been through BUD/s training together. From the moment they'd graduated training, they'd been assigned to Team 10 and hadn't been separated since. The sense of loss hit him hard, weakening his knees. If he'd been alone, he might have given in and dropped. With his commander and Delaney standing close by, he couldn't. He was a SEAL. SEALs didn't show weakness.

He sent a silent prayer to the heavens. God, help Reaper and while you're at it, help me be strong for him. With Delaney at his side, the man would be okay.

Tuck didn't want to think whether or not *he'd* be okay. He couldn't picture Delaney with Reaper. In the back of the Black Hawk helicopter on the way to their mission, he'd convinced himself he couldn't live without her.

Now he'd have to.

Chapter Nine

Cory woke once after the doctors amputated the shattered arm, cleaned his wounds, and packed them with pressure bandages.

Delaney was there when his eyes blinked open three hours later.

"O'Connell?"

"Yeah, Cory. I'm here." She leaned over his bed and smiled downward. The nurses had done a good job bandaging his face. Thankfully, none of the shrapnel had hit his eyes, but he'd have scars on his forehead, nose, cheeks, and chin. They'd just give him more character.

"My arm hurts like hell." He shifted his shoulder and lifted his head to get a look at it.

Delaney touched his chest. "Lie back. I'll talk to the nurse about upping the pain meds." She turned to flag down a nurse.

Cory snagged her arm with his left hand. "Why can't I move my arm?"

Her heart broke as she struggled to come up with the words to tell him he'd never move that arm again.

"What's wrong? Why the sad face? Am I paralyzed?" He lifted the other arm, I.V. tubes and all. "Don't lie to me. Give it to me straight."

She sucked in a deep breath. "The explosion destroyed your right arm. The doctors couldn't save it. They had to..." She couldn't say the word *amputate*.

"They had to remove it."

Cory's brows drew together for a moment, then he lay back, a smile curving his lips. "Is that all? And here I thought the injury was serious." He lay still for a few seconds.

Delaney thought he'd slipped into unconsciousness again until he spoke.

"How's Tuck?"

"He's okay. Took a bullet to the leg. I believe the medics had to sit on him to make him stay still long enough to pull it out."

Cory chuckled once, his brows twisting. "Remind me not to laugh. Hurts. And the others?"

"All the SEALs made it out."

His eyes opened. "Who didn't?"

"The other helicopter crew."

"Damn."

"The main thing is for you to get better. They're moving you soon. You get a first-class plane ride to Landstuhl then back to the States."

"Always wanted to go to Germany," he said, his voice fading.

"Sorry, you won't get to tour this time. Unless you count the inside of the hospital."

"Maybe for our honeymoon."

"About that..." Delaney started, not sure of what she wanted to say. The truth would be best. She turned and paced the length of his bed. "When I agreed to marry you, I wasn't thinking straight. I was worried about you and said what I thought you wanted to hear. The thing is, I love you, but like a brother. So you see, you don't want to marry me. I'm not the right girl for you. You deserve someone who will love you like a husband." Delaney spun to face Cory to gauge his reaction.

He lay as still as death, his breathing shallow, his skin pale from the loss of so much blood. As far as Delaney knew, he hadn't heard a word of her confession.

And as far as she was concerned, he never should. Losing an arm would be hard enough to recover from. Losing an arm and a fiancé at the same time was setting him up to fail. And failure meant death.

Her heart aching, Delaney sat beside Cory, loving him like a brother while she longed for Tuck's arms to be around her, his voice reassuring her everything would be all right.

Captain Swinson stopped beside her. "They're getting ready to move him. If you're going with him, you might want to pack a bag."

Delaney stood and glanced down at Cory.

"Don't worry, I'll stay with him until you get back."

"Thanks." Delaney hugged the other woman and hurried out of the hospital, breathing in the fresh desert air. The sun was just beginning to rise, bathing the camp in a golden haze.

Tired, disheartened, and worried, she hurried to her tent, packed her rucksack with the essentials and a change of uniform, and returned to the hospital. All the way there and back, she glanced around, hoping to catch a glimpse of Tuck.

When she arrived back at the hospital, they had

Cory loaded onto the big wheeled gurney, a medic carrying the IV still attached to his arm. They loaded him into the back of an ambulance and made room for Delaney. She slipped onto a bench next to the medic who hung the IV over the collapsible gurney.

The ride to the helicopter pad passed quickly. Too quickly. Soon, they'd be on their way to Bagram and from there to Landstuhl. She might never see Tuck again, and she hadn't had the opportunity to say goodbye.

At the helicopter pad, the transfer went without a hitch and the pilot shook hands with Delaney. "Heard what happened. Sorry about the crew."

"Me, too."

"I'll try to make the ride as painless as possible."

"Thanks." Delaney climbed on board and behind the pilot, the experience of *riding* in a helicopter so much different than *flying* it.

"Wait!" A shout sounded over the sound of the rotor blades building up speed and one of the medics closed the sliding door.

"Wait!" Across the tarmac, Tuck ran, wearing gym shorts, T-shirt, and tennis shoes, his thick, muscular legs covered in swaths of orange Betadine and patches of stitches. One of the ground crew clotheslined him, bringing him to a halt before he could get close enough to the blades now in motion.

Delaney started to unhook her harness, but the helicopter lifted off, the pilot's focus already on the task ahead, unaware of the man waving frantically. Get the patient to Bagram safely and swiftly. The sooner he got out of the theater, the sooner he'd get the specialized help he'd need to survive.

Helpless to stop the chopper from rising, knowing slowing the trip would only put Cory in more danger, Delaney watched through the scuffed window as Tuck became a tiny dot in the middle of the airfield. Her eyes burned with unshed tears.

Delaney's life was now on a different course. Cory would be her focus until he was well enough to manage on his own.

Chapter Ten

One month later.

"Cory, you have to do it. I can't go back until I know you'll be okay." Delaney stood beside Cory in the large room dedicated to rehabilitation of wounded soldiers.

His face burned red, sweat popping out as he tried to pull the long rubber strap toward him using what was left of his right arm. When it was only halfway, he let go and growled. "Fuck this!"

A pretty blond physical therapist stepped up to him. "Cory, the only way you'll get better is to fight past the pain, and use those muscles that haven't been used in a month. Now do it." Her voice was soft but firm, her lips set in a thin line. Petite and delicate-looking she might be, but she wasn't taking anything less than Cory's best.

"You're new here, aren't you?" Delaney asked.

"Yes, ma'am." She placed the rubber strap over Cory's arm and stepped back. "My name's Leigha. I'll be Cory's physical therapist for the next few weeks."

"I don't want a different therapist," Cory groused. "What was wrong with the one I had?"

"He was transferred to San Antonio Medical Center. He's leaving in two weeks." Leigha nodded toward the rubber strap. "Now, give me five repetitions with the strap."

"I don't have the rest of my arm. Why bother?"

She crossed both arms over her chest and leaned close, whispering, "Are you a SEAL or a pansy ass?"

Delaney was torn between telling off Leigha for being so hard on Cory, and laughing out loud. The woman looked like she could be broken in two by any one of the wounded warriors in the rehab center. She couldn't be more than five feet tall in heels, but she had backbone. In a place as depressing as it was hopeful, she'd need the strength.

Cory had been through multiple surgeries on his stump to clean out the shrapnel, dead tissue, and bone. The pain he'd suffered broke Delaney's heart, and she was glad her commander had given her leave to stay with him through the worst of it.

But now duty called, and she had to go back to the war. After smelling the acrid scents of alcohol and disinfectant, and freezing in hospital rooms kept cool to ward off infection, she looked forward to the grit, dust, and heat of the desert. And she couldn't wait to get back behind the controls of a Black Hawk helicopter.

During one of Cory's rest breaks when his therapist had gone off to help another soldier, Delaney touched his shoulder. "Cory, honey, I need to leave. I have to pack and be on the plane in two hours."

"You sure you don't want me to come with you to the airport?" Cory looked up, his eyebrows raised in a hopeful expression.

Delaney shook her head. "I don't like tearful goodbyes, and I don't want to worry about you getting back to the hospital."

His face fell, and he reached out with his good hand to capture hers. "I don't know what I would have done without you, O'Connell."

She smiled. He'd never called her Delaney and he'd yet to kiss her like he meant it. Sure he'd pecked her on the cheek, but he acted as if he'd lost some of his manhood when he'd lost his arm. As bad as it had been through his surgeries, the agony, and depression, Delaney couldn't tell him how she really felt. After losing an arm, what more disappointment and heartache could he stand?

She really loved Cory and couldn't bear to see him in any additional pain. But did she have to marry him to keep him from giving up hope?

Maybe once she was back in the desert, he'd come to realize they weren't meant to be. And to prove it to him and to herself, she leaned up on her toes to get closer, captured his face between her palms and kissed him like she would have kissed Tuck—long, lingering and with a little tongue action.

Cory didn't taste like Tuck, but he cupped the back of her neck and deepened the kiss. Granted, he was a good kisser. At least, he had that going for him. But the spark just wasn't there—that soul-inspiring jolt of electricity that pulsed through her veins when she kissed Tuck was absent.

"Eh-hem. Want me to come back later?" Leigha stood behind Cory with her brows raised.

Delaney straightened, her cheeks burning. "No. I was just leaving."

"Take your time. I'm here all day." She winked at

Cory and performed a perky about-face.

Delaney chuckled. "I think you've met your match in that one."

"Yeah." Cory frowned, his gaze following the woman across the floor. Then he turned to Delaney. "Promise me you'll Skype when you can."

"I'll try. With the time difference, I'm not sure how often I can."

"And tell Tuck I'm okay. He's probably blaming himself." Cory stared down at his arm. "He shouldn't. I don't."

"I'll let him know." If she saw him in theater. The SEALs didn't always stay in one place for long, and she wasn't sure of her assignment when she got back. They might send her to another province. Her chest ached at the thought of seeing Tuck again. Having left in such a hurry, she hadn't had an opportunity to say all that needed to be said.

Knowing the way Tuck felt about commitment, she wasn't sure there was anything left to say. She was engaged to Cory. Anything they might have had was over unless she broke her engagement.

"Cory?" Delaney opened her mouth, wanting to say so much more. To tell him the kiss hadn't done anything for her, that they weren't meant for each other. To break their engagement.

"Yeah, babe?" He still held her hand, weaving his fingers through hers.

Words lodged in her throat and she finally choked out, "You realize that was our first real kiss."

He smiled. "I know. I'm just sad it wasn't before..." He shrugged. "You know."

"Before you lost your arm?" Delaney called it as it was. "That doesn't matter."

"Does to me. It might have been better."

"The kiss?"

"Yeah."

"You didn't feel anything either?"

His brows furrowed. "Is that what you think?" He pulled her into his one-armed embrace and kissed the top of her head. "Of course I did."

Delaney could have kicked herself. She braced herself for when the full impact of her words came to him.

She didn't have long to wait.

"Wait."

Her stomach sank and knotted.

Cory set her at arm's length, his frown deepening. "Either? Are you telling me you didn't feel it?"

She hesitated, prepared to lie, and then sighed, leaning her forehead against his broad chest. "I wanted to."

He tipped up her chin. "I thought you loved me."

"I do. I'm just not sure it's the kind of love you need."

"O'Connell, I've loved you from the first time you spilled popcorn on the couch in our apartment at Little Creek."

She smiled up at him, his image blurred through a wash of ready tears. "Tuck was mad. He missed a pass by the Miami Dolphins when they played the New England Patriots."

"He got over it. Especially when you started

picking up all the popcorn in his lap. Seems to me he forgot all about the game." Cory grinned. "For a while there, I thought you two would get together."

Delaney opened her mouth to tell him he'd been right.

Before she could, Cory continued. "But when he didn't make a move, I figured I had a shot. So you didn't feel anything when we kissed?" He shook his head. "Then I'm not giving my best." He winked. "I used to have a reputation with the women, until I met you. I had a knack for flirting." His chest puffed out.

"Why did you stop flirting?"

All the air left his lungs and he sagged. "What's it matter? I got my girl. Why should I flirt?"

"Cory, you can't wait around for me. What if I don't come back?"

"You're too damned good a helicopter pilot to bite the big one in the sandbox. You'll be back."

"But—"

"I don't want to hear it. One of us has to carry on the tradition of duty, honor, country."

She pressed a finger to his lips. "Promise me this."

He captured the finger and kissed the tip. "Anything."

"Keep your options open."

He frowned. "I love you, O'Connell. I don't want anything else."

"Promise me," she insisted, narrowing her gaze.

"I'll think about it."

She waited, ready to blurt out that she wanted to be released from her promise to marry him, but at the last minute couldn't. "Play nice with your therapist and be strong."

"I have to be. We're getting married when you get back." He drew her close with his good arm and crushed her lips with his.

Delaney let him kiss her, allowing his tongue to slide between her teeth and caress the length of hers. When they broke apart, she only felt relief. Ducking her head, she hurried from the room, casting one last glance behind her as she left.

Cory was still watching her, his brow furrowed.

Leigha, the therapist, descended on him and put him to work.

At least he was in good hands. Leigha knew what Cory needed more than Delaney. With her out of the way, he'd work hard at recuperating. When she returned, she'd break the truth to him that they couldn't get married. By that time, he'd have had weeks apart from her. Hopefully enough time to see that they weren't right for each other.

Her heart heavy, Delaney struck out for her hotel room to pack her bag and take a taxi to the airport. Her pulse quickened at the thought of being back in the cockpit and in the same country as Tuck.

*

"I heard Razor is back in town."

Tuck was on his seventieth sit-up when Big Bird dropped that bomb. He stopped halfway up, his heart slamming hard against his chest. Delaney was back. "That's good." He pumped out ten more repetitions, sweat dripping off his brow. Though the sun was well on its way to the horizon, the earth had yet to lose any of the daytime residual heat. Temperatures hovered at over one hundred, until the sun completely set. And then the sandbox became almost bearable.

Big Bird dropped down beside him and started with leg lifts, making them look like child's play, his long legs rising and falling, the muscles of his bare abdomen flexing and extending with each rep.

"Read on Reaper's Facebook he was doing good. Got him in rehab. Bet he's givin' those therapists a run for their money. Should be bench pressing a couple hundred pounds by day three."

Tuck remained silent, his gut clenching.

Big Bird let his feet fall to the ground and he stared over at Tuck. "You still thinking the injury was your fault?"

Tuck grunted, refusing to answer. His team never missed an opportunity to counsel him on what he should and shouldn't be feeling. He'd been there when Cory had almost lost his life.

"Could have been any one of us. Even you."

"Should have been me," he bit out, regretting his outburst as soon as it crossed his lips.

"We all signed on as SEALs, accepting the risks equally. Just because you didn't go through that door first doesn't mean you got something to be ashamed of."

"I don't want to talk about it." Tuck rose to his feet, ready to jog a dozen laps inside the wire. Outside the wire, if he could. To hell with IEDs. Maybe he'd land on one and put an end to his second-guessing.

Big Bird rose, lightning fast, and grabbed his arm.

"Well, you better talk about something. We're a team, and you're not acting like a part of it."

Tuck's fists clenched. He wanted to hit Big Bird, a man he'd give his life for. Hell, there wasn't a man on his entire team he wouldn't give his life for. Including Reaper.

"Go ahead, hit me," Big Bird said. "If punching me makes you feel better and gets this shit outta your system. We need you back, one hundred ten percent. You copy?"

His fists loosened and he nodded. "Roger."

Big Bird let go of his arm and stepped back. "Now, run. Sweat it out and be ready for our next call."

Tuck took off and ran. And ran. After four laps around the perimeter, he'd pushed himself so hard he probably bordered on heat exhaustion. He stumbled to the shower tent and stood under the lukewarm water until his body cooled enough to ensure he wouldn't pass out.

Big Bird had been right. He'd been in a cross between raging funk and a shit hole since Reaper had been medevaced out with a CCATT team and Delaney. Time for him to get his head on straight and did what he'd trained to do. Kill the bad guys.

He dried off and stepped into a pair of clean shorts, slipped on his flip-flops, and shook the water out of his shaggy hair. He might even get a haircut. That might make him feel more human, less like a slug.

With his attitude adjusted, he stepped out of the shower tent and ran into Captain Delaney O'Connell, nearly knocking her off her feet.

She staggered backward until he caught her arm and dragged her against his chest.

"Tuck." Her face blanched at first, then flushed.

"Delaney." His fingers tightened around her arm, his mouth twitching, aching to claim hers. A knot lodged in his gut.

Her gaze shifted to his mouth and her pretty pink tongue darted out to wet her lips.

He wanted to taste where her tongue had been, to chew on that full lower lip, to suck it into his mouth while his hand roved over her body.

She wore a robe and he'd bet not much underneath, and his fingers itched to explore and find out if her skin was really as soft as he remembered.

Tuck dipped his head, his mouth angling toward hers. "I'd heard you were back."

She tipped back her head, her eyes drifting to half-mast. "I missed you."

Before his lips touched hers, he remembered. Tuck straightened, his hand falling to his sides. "How's Cory?" He backed up several steps, afraid to be too close in case he forgot himself again.

"Doing better. He's in rehab now. The worst of the surgeries are over, and he's on his way to mending."

"That's good." Pulling his towel from his shoulder, he stretched the damp terry cloth between his fists, anything to keep from reaching out and pulling her into his arms again. "How was your flight back?"

Her mouth twisted into a wry grin. "Long and

tedious."

Every instinct urged him to grab this woman and kiss her until they were both breathless. He'd really missed her. More than he'd ever missed any woman. But she was taken.

"Well, I'm glad you made it back safely and that Cory is doing better." He turned to walk away before he did something stupid. A SEAL didn't lust after his buddy's fiancé.

"Tuck?" A soft touch on his arm stopped him, a crackle of electricity shooting through his veins. He froze, fighting the urge to throw her over his shoulder and find a quiet, shadowed space where he could make mad, crazy love to her in this camp full of soldiers.

He stared down at her hand, willing her to remove it.

She didn't, the fingers tightening. "I missed you," she said softly.

"You're with Cory now." His voice came out harsh, unyielding.

She looked away. "The injury's been hard on him. For a man so used to doing everything himself, he's had to rely on others."

His heart ached for his friend. If he could have, he'd have gone with them to the States and done everything in his power to help Cory through the worst of it. In a softer tone, he said, "I'm glad you were there with him."

She looked up, her eyes glassy with unshed tears. "I had to be. But I wanted to be here. With you." Her chin dipped, and a single tear slipped down her cheek.

That tear was Tuck's undoing. He pulled her into his arms and crushed her to him. "Jesus, Del. I never knew how much I'd miss you until you were gone. Four weeks felt like four years."

"I'm here now." Her hand curled around the back of his neck.

He bent to take her lips, stopping just short. Then he gripped her face between his palms, his jaw hardening. "You know we can't do this."

She stared into his eyes, her own, limpid pools. "Why does facing a hundred enemy soldiers seem easy compared to this?" She laughed and brushed a tear from the corner of her eyes.

"I can't do this."

She nodded. "I know."

"Our relationship has to be strictly business from now on."

Again, she nodded, swallowing hard, more tears streaming down her face.

"Goodnight, Captain O'Connell." Against his better judgment, he pressed a kiss to her forehead. The gesture wasn't enough to make up for what he really wanted from her. But Cory was a long way from recovery and would never get back his arm. Tuck hadn't saved him from losing it in the first place, he sure as hell wasn't going to be responsible for Cory losing Delaney.

He turned and walked away from the only woman he'd felt he could have loved enough to spend the rest of his life with.

For several minutes, Delaney stood where he'd

left her, unable to move for the tears blinding her. She'd never cried over a man...until Tuck. Damn him!

She scrubbed the tears from her cheeks, but more followed. If she didn't get a grip on her emotions, one of her squad members would see her. Then word would get back the female Night Stalker was going all hormonal and losing her touch. She refused to let her personal life interfere with her professional duties. Squaring her shoulders, though her heart hurt enough to make her sick to her stomach, she completed her shower and headed back to the tent she shared with Lindsay.

"You don't look much better for the shower," the nurse commented when she entered the tent.

"I'm not here to win a beauty contest," Delaney mumbled, turning away so that Lindsay couldn't see her puffy eyes and guess that she'd been crying.

"So, did you run into tall, dark and gorgeous?"

Delaney's lips twitched. "If you're referring to Tuck, yes. I saw him briefly."

"Is he disappointed you are engaged to another man?"

"Apparently not."

"Did he try to kiss you?"

"Not even once. He'd never poach on a buddy's territory."

Lindsay sighed. "Must be nice to have two handsome SEALs in love with you at once."

"No, it's not." Delaney fell onto her cot and buried her face in her pillow. She'd been so happy to see Tuck. For him to keep her at a distance was killing her.

"Captain O'Connell?" a voice spoke from outside her tent.

She sat up, scrubbed her hands over her face to wash away all traces of tears then said, "Enter."

A young PFC stepped through the doorway. "Your presence is required in the Ops tent in fifteen minutes."

Delaney thanked the PFC and waited until he left before groaning.

"Holy smokes, you've barely been here half a day and they're sending you out?"

Delaney didn't care. Anywhere was better than staying in the same camp as Tuck. Vowing to be tough, she suited up, grabbed her flight bag, and marched to the Ops tent.

The next couple days passed in a blur of flying sorties and getting back up to speed on the ongoing effort to suppress the Taliban insurgents wreaking havoc on nearby villages.

She didn't see Tuck, nor have anything to do with SEAL operations during that time frame. Two weeks passed, and she still hadn't run into Tuck. She figured he was avoiding her. Accepting the fact he didn't want anything to do with her, she went about her business, flying sorties of troops and supplies to the hard-to-reach or dangerous locations in the enemy-infested hills.

During the second week she was back, she got orders to conduct a night mission heading north into cave-pocked hills. The operations hut had been sweltering hot and tempers had been short. She and her crew were supposed to deliver a small squad of highly trained troops to a building. Then she was to hover nearby until she got word from the soldiers to extract them. She'd done this type of maneuver so many times, she could almost fly it blind, although that wasn't advisable.

That evening, she showed up at the chopper, performed all her flight checks, and settled into the pilot's seat.

The crew climbed on board, checked their weapons, and gave her the verbal "thumbs up". A group of men showed up dressed all in black, including their black Kevlar vests and helmets. Each face was smeared in black camouflage, unrecognizable, but by their sizes and shapes, she recognized the members of the SEAL Unit, assigned to Camp Leatherneck.

Delaney's heart thumped against her chest. She wondered if Tuck was one of the SEALs dressed in black. Would he speak to her, if he was? Perhaps not knowing and not talking to him was better. He was just another troop who needed a skilled pilot to insert and extract him from the designated locations.

Keeping her focus forward, she checked her gauges and waited for her cue from the gunners in back.

"Take her up!" Mac called out.

Easing back on the control, she lifted off the ground and sent the helicopter toward their destination.

The flight went smoothly with little radio chatter, and soon Delaney hovered low over the drop zone.

SEALs fast-roped to the ground and ran toward what appeared to be dark holes in the sides of the hills.

Before they'd gone twenty yards, the bright flare of tracer rounds lit the insides of one of the black entrances to the mountainside.

Delaney had been briefed to take off immediately and retreat to a safe location away from the firefight. Yet, she hesitated, afraid the bullets being fired would hit one of the SEALs rushing toward the caves.

She started to pull up when the door gunner let loose a round of fifty-caliber bullets. "Man down!" he shouted into his mic. "Man down!"

Delaney lifted off the ground and swooped in, aiming at the opening where the tracer rounds blinked in the dark.

"What are you doing?" her co-pilot asked.

"Rescuing an American," she said, her fingers tight on the controls, her insides quaking. The man down could be Tuck.

"They have to take out the gunner before we can pick them up. We're one giant target out here, captain."

"We can't leave a man down."

"No, but we can't help if we're shot down."

Hovering a moment longer, she forced her hand to move. The helicopter pulled up and back, flying away from the action.

Delaney goosed the fuel, sending the chopper leaping upward.

"Incoming!" Mac cried.

An explosion rocked the entire craft and it

pitched to the starboard, heading straight into a rocky hillside.

Delaney fought for control, righting the blades at the last minute, but not soon enough to miss the bullets strafing the fuselage.

"Shit! I'm hit," Jones called out.

Not only was Jones hit, the helicopter shuddered, the engine shut down, and they plummeted toward earth.

"Brace yourselves for an emergency landing!" Delaney said into mic. With the power off, the blades slowed and gravity did the rest.

Chapter Eleven

Tuck was halfway up the hill to the cave where the RPG had launched a grenade and the machine gun was hammering his men. He refused to look back, his goal was to stop the bleeding and neutralize the threat.

Positioning himself close enough to make the enemy think twice, and also close enough to be shot at, Tuck laid down suppressive fire while Big Bird aimed his grenade launcher at the cave entrance and lobbed a high-explosive grenade into the gaping maw.

Tuck took cover.

The explosion spewed debris in a thirty-foot radius outside the cave entrance, raining down gravel. With a shake, Tuck picked himself up off the ground and rushed the entrance, slipping in the side.

The machine gunner lay in the rubble, the gun nothing but parts and scattered unexpended rounds. Movement at the back of the cave and a moan sent Tuck deeper.

"I'm behind you," Big Bird's voice whispered through the headset affixed to the inside of Tuck's helmet.

With his teammate at his back, Tuck adjusted his NVGs and eased toward the back where tunnels branched off the main entrance. Great, which way? His goggles picked up green dots of a warm trail on the ground. Fresh blood, leading to the right.

Tuck waited for Big Bird to catch up, then he followed the trail deeper into the mountain.

A flash of green ahead kicked up his pulse. He ducked lower, aimed his weapon and charged forward to catch up.

Sounds alerted him to more than one enemy ahead. He slowed, dropped to his belly and low crawled, using his elbows, around the corner. Six rifles pointed where his chest would have been.

He fired at their knees, expending all thirty rounds in his clip.

Big Bird lay down beside him and fired.

Tuck jettisoned the clip and slammed another in its place. Before he pulled the trigger to continue his assault, he focused on the six men lying on the ground in front of him. Two still moved; the others lay still.

Bringing his knees up beneath him, Tuck hurried forward, ready to dive to the left or right should one raise a weapon.

The two still alive thrashed and moaned.

A grenade rolled out at Tuck's feet. "Get back!" he yelled.

Big Bird, still holding the corner, scooted back around the rock wall.

Tuck sprinted and dove into the tunnel, then rolled around the corner as the explosion erupted around them. The ground beneath him bucked and rocks from the ceiling pummeled his back. Dust filled the air and choked his lungs.

Tuck's ears rang and he could barely stand without staggering.

Big Bird was around here somewhere amongst the rubble.

His NVGs lost in the stones and dust, Tuck felt in his pockets for the mini flashlight he carried, praying it still worked, or he'd have a helluva time finding his way back out of the tunnel. A click sounded near him, and light caught the flying dust particles, making a strange glow.

"Tuck?" Big Bird's voice sounded like it came through the thick glass bottom of a soda bottle. He shone the light in Tuck's eyes, his M4 aimed at Tuck's chest.

"Yeah, I'm okay, but I can't hear worth a crap. Don't get trigger happy." Tuck pushed away the nose of his weapon and clicked on his own flashlight. "Come on. We need to find the rest of the men."

They retraced their steps back to the cave entrance.

Fish, Gator, and Dustman were nowhere to be seen. Flames rose from a dark structure lying on the ground halfway across the valley.

For a moment, Tuck didn't make the connection.

Big Bird backhanded him in the gut. "Ain't that our chopper?"

Tuck leaped off the ledge of the cave and ran, slid, scooted down the steep hillside to the bottom. Without slowing, he ran, all out, across the desert valley.

Big Bird yelled behind him. "Tuck! Don't be stupid. You're of no use to anyone dead."

Tuck barely heard him, the humming in his ears blocking most sound from reaching his brain. The chopper was down, on fire, and Delaney had been the pilot. "Fuck!" He ran faster.

Behind him, Big Bird yelled, "Don't shoot! It's us!"

Gator and Fish stepped out from behind the wreckage as Tuck reeled into the light from the burning aviation fuel. "Survivors?" he gasped.

"The door gunners took bullets and they're pretty banged up, and the co-pilot busted a leg."

Tuck grabbed Gator's Kevlar vest and jerked him close. "The pilot?"

Gator shook his head.

His heart plummeting, Tuck shoved Gator away. "Where is she?"

"Tuck, she's alive, but she must be bleeding internally. She's been unconscious since we pulled her out of the helicopter."

"Where...is...she?" He rounded the craft to the other side where the injured crew members and Dustman lay scattered across the ground. All of them greeted him with a raised hand, except one.

She lay on the hard-packed dirt, her helmet and electronic kneeboard on the ground beside her.

Tuck dropped down at her side and placed his ear near her mouth, listening for breathing, feeling for the blessed release of air from between those beautiful lips.

A hand settled on his shoulder. "Tuck, she's breathing and her pulse is slow but steady."

Tuck glanced up at Gator. "Dustman?"

"Took a round in the thigh. He went down, but was up again a couple minutes later."

"I think she hesitated when I went down," Dustman said.

Tuck brushed a long sandy blond hair off her cheek and said softly, "Knucklehead."

Gator, the big man from Louisiana, with the tattoos of an alligator and a swamp rat on his biceps and hair down around his shoulders, looked like a wild man from the swamps. But he was one of the best SEALs Tuck had ever had on his side. He stood straight, weapon ready, scanning the hillside above him. "I've radioed for backup. We're to sit tight, hold our position, and keep these guys safe."

Fish asked, "Did you get 'em?"

Tuck nodded, the attack's success inconsequential compared to what had happened outside the cave.

He stayed with Delaney while Gator and Fish set up a perimeter around the crashed helicopter. Each minute ticked by like hours until finally the whopping sound of helicopter rotors rose in the distance. Minutes later, two helicopters landed. Medics leaped to the ground, carrying bags of medical equipment and stretchers.

A very short time later, they were on their way back to Camp Leatherneck.

After Tuck saw to the safety of his team, he gave the medics all the room they needed, but insisted on riding in the same aircraft as Delaney.

They'd strapped her to a board, immobilizing her in case she'd suffered neck or spinal injuries. An I.V. drip fed fluid into her veins and an oxygen mask was secured to her face. She looked small in the mass of equipment and crowds of men in uniforms.

Tuck had never felt more frustrated and useless than at that moment. He wanted her to wake up so he could tell her to hang on. That he loved her and that if she didn't marry Cory, and married him instead, he'd be the happiest man on the planet.

He managed to hold her hand the entire flight back and helped carry the stretcher to the camp's hospital where the doctors and nurses took over.

Once Delaney was out of sight, Tuck checked on Dustman. He'd been giving his female surgeon a hard time, refusing to have her administer a local anesthetic while she fished for the slug. He insisted on being strapped down and then proceeded to tell her he was enjoying it. Not amused, the surgeon fished the bullet out of his leg, sewed him up, and pumped him full of fluid and antibiotics.

"And get the hell out of my hospital in the morning." After giving him strict instructions to stay off the leg until then, she left his side, tossing a wink over her shoulder.

"How's Delaney?" Dustman asked, wiping the sweat off his brow with the white sheet gathered around his middle.

"I don't know."

Dustman's hand stilled. "You don't know? And you've parked your raggedy ass here? What's wrong with you?" He leaned over, shoved Tuck, and winced. "Go, before I bust a stitch and get Brunhilde von Shaft riding my ass again."

By the time he got back to the door Delaney disappeared through, Captain Lindsay Swinson was there, worried wrinkles on her forehead. "You're Tuck, aren't you?"

When he nodded, she smiled, hooked his arm, and dragged him to another section of the hospital where beds lined the walls, many of them empty. At the far end of the room, one had a body in it. As he neared, he recognized the sandy blond hair.

Delaney lay as still as death, her face pale, almost chalky in appearance.

His knees shook and he almost fell. "Is she okay?"

"The doc said she was a little messed up inside. He had to remove damaged tissue."

Tuck's fists clenched. "Will she be okay?"

Swinson nodded, a smile spilling across her face. After a moment, the smile disappeared. "The doctors said she sustained damage to her uterus." The nurse paused and finished in a rush. "They did what they could, but she may never have children."

"Who cares? She almost died. If she lives, that will be enough." He dragged in a deep breath. "When I saw the helicopter in flames..."

"She's tough. She'll pull through." Swinson sighed. "I'll miss her as a roommate."

Miss her? His body went rigid. "What do you mean?"

"No one told you?"

"Told me what?"

"Tomorrow, they're putting her on a plane back to the States." The nurse stared at him. "Are you going to be all right?"

"I'm fine." No, he wasn't fine. His world was

falling apart, he was stuck in this desert shit hole when Delaney was going back stateside. If something happened to her while he was here...

"Since she doesn't have any family, they're sending her to Bethesda to be with her fiancé during her recuperation."

The weight of her words slammed into his chest, making it hard for him to breathe.

"You love her, don't you?" the nurse asked.

Did he love Delaney? As soon as he thought the question, the answer was as clear as it was painful, and it had been there from the first time they'd shared a pizza.

With every beat of his heart, he loved her.

Nurse Swinson chuckled. "You don't have to answer. I can see it in your face." Her smile turned to a frown. "If you love her, why are you letting her marry another guy?"

"You don't understand."

"What don't I understand?"

"Reaper's my friend." He scrubbed a hand through his hair. "A guy doesn't poach on his buddy's girl. Especially when he's going through hard times."

"What about Delaney?"

The words formed like sand in his mouth but he said them anyway. "She chose him."

"And she's miserable."

"Delaney's aircraft was shot down. Anyone would be miserable."

"Don't be thickheaded, frogman." Swinson shook her head. "Miserable in love with you. Doesn't that mean anything to you?"

His gut clenched like he'd been sucker punched. "What did you not understand about *she chose him*?"

"She doesn't love him in that way."

"He lost his fuckin' arm. I'm not takin' his girl."

"You're both so stubborn, you're going to let this mistake go forward?"

"There's nothing I can do to stop it. It's all in Cory's hands." He closed his eyes, his friend's pain washing over him. "Hand."

Swinson sighed. "Then you're all fools."

He glanced down at Delaney.

She looked so pale that his stomach clenched. "When is she supposed to wake up?"

"When her body is ready."

"Will she wake before she leaves in the morning?"

"We don't know. From what we *do* know, her helicopter landed hard. So far she's not showing any swelling on the brain, but it is a possibility."

"Can I stay here with her?"

"If it's all right with your commanding officer, you can stay all night. I'll get a chair, but it won't be comfortable."

"I don't need comfort." He needed Delaney to wake up so that he could tell her.

Tell her what? That he loved her? That she couldn't marry Reaper and that he couldn't live without her?

Maybe it was just as well Delaney slept through the night. By morning when the medevac folks came, she hadn't come to.

When they moved her to the transport stretcher,

she stirred. "Tuck?"

He was there, holding her hand. "I'm here," he reassured her, walking with the team of medical personnel carrying her to the ambulance that would take her to the airfield.

"You're okay." Her eyelids drifted closed as if they were too heavy to hold open.

"Yes, I am."

A smile tipped the corners of her lips.

Then she whispered so softly he had to bend close to hear. "I love you." He pressed a kiss to her lips and before he could do more, they loaded her into a helicopter bound for Bagram, then Landstuhl, and ultimately back to Bethesda where she'd be reunited with Reaper, her fiancé.

As the helicopter lifted from the ground, Tuck felt as if his heart had been ripped from his chest. He couldn't stand by and watch his best friend marry the woman he loved, and he couldn't bust them up. Not when his friend had lost so much. Torn so completely, he could lie around and wallow in his self-pity, which was not something he tolerated in others, or he could do something to take his mind off his troubles.

Tuck marched to his commander's tent, still wearing the black combat uniform of the night before, dusty, dirty and probably smelling like a wet dog.

"Tuck, how's the chopper pilot?" Commander Janek settled a cap over his head and stepped outside into the morning heat.

"On her way to the States. She'll live." With

Reaper. Tuck's fists clenched and his heart squeezed so tightly in his chest he thought he was having a heart attack. "I want to go after the Taliban informer who set us up last night and the mission that cost Reaper his arm."

His commander stood still, staring into Tuck's face. "What have you heard?"

"I understand intel got a lead on him."

Janek nodded. "I'm assembling a team today."

"I want in on it."

The skipper's brows knitted. "Are you sure you're up to the task?"

Straightening his shoulders, Tuck stood tall. "Always."

"We'll talk after you've had a shower. You stink." Janek turned toward the mess tent, hesitated, and turned back. "This mission will be the most dangerous one you've ever been on. It will require living in the worst conditions for long periods of time and being cut off from civilization for weeks."

Perfect. He wouldn't be around for Reaper and Delaney's wedding. "The longer the better."

One month later.

"Are you sure this is how you want to do this? You don't want to have it in a church surrounded by all your buddies from SEAL Team 10?" Delaney was dressed in a pretty cream-colored dress, her hair pulled back and up with tiny rhinestone butterflies clipped throughout. She looked better than she'd ever looked, and her heart raced in anticipation of the events about to take place.

"Humor me, will ya?" Cory waved his stump of an arm, the surgical scars thick and ragged. "I'll have the people who mean the most to me here."

Delaney was happy he'd finally gotten the phantom pain under control. The first few weeks after the explosion had been hell with nerve synapses that used to lead to his now-missing arm firing off messages to his brain that translated into agonizing pain. His cries had nearly broken Delaney's heart. She'd been there as much as possible. Ultimately, the nurses caring for him took center stage, then the physical therapists. One in particular.

When she'd arrived at Bethesda, she'd been too out of it to know what was going on. The doctors had been the best, and she'd recovered within a couple weeks, enough to visit Cory at his therapy session.

She couldn't believe the change in the month since she'd left. They'd really turned his entire attitude around since the beginning, and she was thankful. He'd been so upbeat, she barely recognized him from the sour-faced, angry man of before. His new lease on life centered around one therapist.

Once she was sufficiently recovered, Delaney had been reassigned to temporary duty at the Pentagon as executive staff to Joint Chiefs of Staff, reviewing the Joint Air Operations Publication. Her commander had stressed the duty was only temporary until she passed the flight physical, at which time she'd be reassigned to duty with the 160th SOAR.

Battling both the D.C. traffic and the Metro

reminded her of why she liked deployment. Fighting the Taliban and being shot at seemed less stressful than rush-hour traffic. She looked forward to getting back in the cockpit. Healed and rested, she was ready.

Today was Cory's last day at Bethesda, and his wedding day. She couldn't be happier. Well, she could, but that was another story and one she'd closed the book on the day she'd flown out of Camp Leatherneck in the back of the Black Hawk to Bagram.

So much had happened. So many things had changed. But one thing was clear, Tuck hadn't come looking for her, hadn't tried to contact her or see her, or even Skype her from the field.

On many occasions, Cory had tried to reach him online. He'd finally given up and contacted their commander to learn Tuck was out on a special mission. He'd left word with their commander with the date of his wedding and that he was saving the spot of best man for Tuck. Be there.

Now Delaney stood beside Cory in the ward where he'd performed most of his physical therapy, surrounded by the therapists, doctors, and nurses who'd seen him through the worst of his recovery.

Someone pressed the button on an MP3 player and Mendelssohn's *Wedding March* filled the room.

Cory waved his stump. "Wait. He's not here yet."

"Who's not here?" Delaney asked, a niggle of suspicion running up her back.

"My best man. He promised he'd be here on time. His plane landed over an hour ago. He should be here by now."

The door to the therapy room crashed open, and a tall man dressed in the U.S. Navy service dress blue uniform burst through. "Am I too late?"

Delaney's heart skipped several beats then crashed against her chest, banging like a bass drum in a parade. "Tuck?"

"Tuck! You made it!" Cory wagged his stump. "About damned time. The ceremony's about to start. Get up here."

From ten feet away, Tuck stared from Cory to Delaney, his gaze fixing on her. "I wasn't going to come, but Skipper insisted."

"Not come to my wedding?" Cory grinned, his spirit indomitable on his wedding day. "You'd skip out on seeing your best bud shackled with an old ball and chain?"

"She's not a ball and chain. Any man would be proud to have her as his wife." His words were for Cory, but his gaze centered on Delaney.

Her heart thumped hard against his ribs. Delaney bit her lip to keep the tears from falling. The pain did little to stop them, and several slipped down her cheek. "Cory, you didn't tell me he was coming."

"I know." Cory winked at her. "I wanted to surprise you." In a stronger voice, he addressed Tuck. "Are you standing by me or do I have to ask Schotzy to fill in?"

A large man in scrubs stepped forward. "I'd be happy to."

"Stand down. Let the man decide first." Cory faced Tuck. "What's it to be? You've been my best friend since BUD/s. I don't want to do this without

158

you by my side, but I will."

"I came to stop this wedding." Tuck came forward.

The people gathered in the room emitted a collective gasp.

Delaney almost laughed at the comical expression on Cory's face.

"Why would you stop me from marrying the girl I love?"

Big hands drew into fists at Tuck's sides. "Because you can't marry her."

"Why? Is she already married and I didn't know?"

"No." Tuck's face darkened, getting more fierce with each passing second.

"She agreed to marry me. I love her." Cory waved his good hand to the side. "What more confirmation do I need?"

"She doesn't love you," Tuck blurted.

"That's news to me," a female voice called out from a side door. She stepped through wearing a simple white wedding dress that hugged her figure perfectly. Her long blond hair hung down her back, straight and shiny, unlike the unruly mass of sandy blond curls Delaney fought to control with ponytails and hairclips.

Tuck stared, his mouth dropping open. "Who's she?"

"Uh, Tuck..." Delaney fought the smile spreading across her lips. "You've been in dark ops too long. I take it you haven't talked to Cory in a while, and there's been a...uh...change of plan."

"I don't understand. I came to stop you from

making the biggest mistake of my life."

"The biggest mistake of *your* life?" Cory asked. "And what would that be?"

"Marrying Delaney."

Delaney lifted her chin and hooked her arm through Cory's elbow. "I happen to think Cory would make a terrific husband." She nodded toward the woman at the far side of the room, slowly working her way toward them. "A terrific husband for Leigha."

"Who's Leigha?" Tuck demanded.

"Shh." Leigha pressed a finger to her lips and picked up the pace, marching up to Tuck. "Please stop yelling. You're disturbing the patients."

Cory grinned and stared around the room at the medical staff and patients in attendance. "Are we disturbing anyone?"

As one, they shouted. "No!"

"Marry her, already!" A triple amputee in a wheelchair shouted. "We want to see the kiss."

"I don't understand." Tuck turned toward Delaney.

She smiled and took pity on him. "Cory's marrying Leigha, his physical therapist."

"I came to stop him from marrying *you*," Tuck said, looking more befuddled by the minute.

"You're a little late for that. We broke our engagement shortly after O'Connell arrived at Bethesda. You'd know this fact if you hadn't gone off all dark ops on us." Cory shook his head as if Tuck was a thick-headed child who had to be taught the same thing more than once before it sank in. "O'Connell doesn't love me."

160

"Yes, I do." Delaney chuckled and pecked Cory's cheek. "Like a brother. And since he doesn't have any siblings or relatives, someone had to look out for his well-being."

As she approached Tuck, the woman in the wedding dress stuck out her hand. "I'm Leigha. You must be Tuck." She grinned. "You're just like Cory described you."

Tuck's brows descended into a blazing frown directed at Cory. "And when were you going to tell me you two had called it off?"

"I'd have told you sooner, if I'd known you cared." Cory glared back at his friend. "But you seemed hell-bent on volunteering for every suicide mission they could come up with. And you never returned any of my messages. I figured you had some bug up your ass about her."

"So you fell in love with Leigha?"

Cory smiled. "I did." He held out his good hand.

Leigha joined him and curled her hand around his bandaged arm. "I didn't like him at first. He was very grouchy. Then when we got the pain under control, he turned out to be such a flirt with all the ladies. I had a hard time trusting him."

"She fell for my charm and good looks." Cory smiled down at her. "And the tattoo of Daisy Mae on my ass."

"No, I fell and you helped me up with your injured arm, even though I knew it hurt like hell." She shook her head, a sweet smile playing across her lips. "I figured if you could sacrifice a little pain to help me up, you couldn't be all bad. Maybe half bad. And that's just the way I like you. Half bad boy, half gentleman. One hundred percent SEAL." She stood on tiptoe and kissed him full on the lips. "Now, are you marrying me or do I have to return this dress for a refund?"

"Let's have a wedding!" Cory shouted.

They skipped the wedding march and got straight to the *I do's*. Soon the room was full of chatter and laughter and people eating cake.

Delaney fought hard not to stare at Tuck. Her heart sang with the joy of having him there, in the same room, and her mind whirred with a thousand questions she wanted to ask. Number one being, why did he come to stop the wedding he thought was between her and Cory? With everyone around them, congratulating Cory and Leigha, she wasn't sure when or if she'd get a chance to be alone with Tuck. Hell, she was a Night Stalker pilot, known for her fearlessness. Then why was she shaking in her heels at the thought of a confrontation with the man she loved?

Tuck stood beside Cory throughout the nuptials, his head spinning with the change in direction. He'd fought coming and wouldn't have, if the Skipper hadn't ordered him to do the right thing and show up for his best friend's wedding.

Once committed to attending, he'd convinced himself he had to stop the wedding. Delaney didn't love Cory and she shouldn't marry him out of pity. Now that he was there, and Cory was married to Leigha...

He finally glanced across the room at Delaney and his chest squeezed so tight he could barely breathe. She was so beautiful in her cream-colored lace dress, she was as pretty as the bride. No.

Delaney was the most beautiful woman he'd ever known. Inside and out. Brave, caring, and gutsy, she was the kind of woman he could picture himself spending the rest of his life getting to know even better.

Then what the hell was he waiting for?

He marched across the room, closing the distance between them.

She glanced up from the plate of cake she had been picking at and their gazes met. Her fork grew still.

When he reached her, he took the plate from her hands and laid it on a nearby table. "Why did you break your engagement to Cory?"

"What does it matter?" She shrugged, her gaze dipping to where his hands held hers. "He loves Leigha and she loves him."

"Do you love him more than a brother?" His fingers squeezed hers and he held his breath, waiting for her response.

"No." She laughed softly. "Though Cory would make a great husband, I made the error of falling in love with someone else."

Tuck dared to hope and his heart pounded. "And you're afraid this guy you love isn't good husband material?" He tugged her toward him.

"I know for a fact he's terrible husband material." Her voice caught on a sob and she looked up, tears swimming in her eyes. "But I can't help it. I love him."

"Then why don't you tell him?"

"I don't know how he feels about me." Her gaze dropped to the buttons on his chest.

Tuck lifted her chin. "I love you so much, not even an entire army of Taliban could erase you from my mind."

"You tried to erase me from your mind?" A tear slipped down her cheek. "See? You make terrible husband material." She swiped at the tear and tried to push away from him.

His grip tightened. "Oh, baby. I may not say the right words, but my heart's in the right place."

"Yeah, and where's that?"

"In your hands." He crushed her against his chest and buried his face in her hair. "I love you, Delaney O'Connell. More than I love living. And I want you in my life, as my wife. What do you say?"

"Is that a marriage proposal?" She leaned back in his arms, staring wide-eyed up at him, more tears spilling down her cheeks.

He pushed the curls behind her ears and kissed the tip of her nose, then thumbed the tears off her skin. "Oh, sweetheart, did I louse that up too? Yes, that was a marriage proposal. But here, let me do it right."

He set her away from him and dropped to one knee, fishing in his pocket for a square box he'd picked up at the duty-free shop in the airport. He opened it, took out the sapphire and diamond ring inside, and held it out. "Delaney O'Connell, will you marry this lousy excuse for husband material? I promise to try my best to make you happy."

"About time, man." Cory clapped his hand on Tuck's back. "I thought you'd never ask. So, O'Connell, are you marrying this suicidal dumbass, or not?"

Air lodged in Tuck's throat as he balanced on one knee, waiting for her response. The wait was harder than anything he'd experienced in BUD/s training.

At first, tears dribbled down her cheeks and her lips trembled.

Tuck fought hard to keep calm when his world could easily fall apart if the woman he loved refused his offer. Time stood still, his heart stopped beating, and sweat broke out across his forehead.

Then she threw her arms around him, crying, "Yes!"

He staggered backward, righted himself, and stood, wrapping his arm around her so tightly he thought she might break.

This woman who could fly into enemy territory, probably kick the asses of most men and could drink whiskey like nobody's business, while looking so feminine she was the envy of every woman, could have any man she wanted.

And she'd chosen him.

She laughed and kissed him. "How will we make this work? I'm not giving up my position in the 160th and you're a SEAL."

He swung her around. "I don't know, but we'll find a way."

"It won't be easy."

"Babe, I relish the challenge, because you're the one I love and want to be with." He glanced over his head at Reaper and winked. "Besides, easy is overrated, and the only easy day was yesterday."

THE END

About the Author

Elle James *also writing as Myla Jackson* spent twenty years livin' and lovin' in South Texas, ranching horses, cattle, goats, ostriches and emus. A former IT professional, Elle is proud to be writing full-time, penning intrigues and paranormal adventures that keep her readers on the edge of their seats. Now living in northwest Arkansas, she isn't wrangling cattle, she's wrangling her muses, a malti-poo and yorkie. When she's not at her computer, she's traveling, out snow-skiing, boating, or riding her ATV, dreaming up new stories.

To learn more about Elle James and her stories visit her website at http://www.ellejames.com.

To learn more about Myla Jackson visit her websites at www.mylajackson.com

Take No Prisoners Series
Book Two

SEAL'S
Desire

New York Times & USA Today Bestselling Author
ELLE JAMES

SEAL's Desire

Take No Prisoners Series
Book #2

Elle James

New York Times Bestselling Author

Take No Prisoners Series
SEAL's Honor (#1)
SEAL's Desire (#2)
SEAL's Embrace (#3)
SEAL's Obsession (#4)
SEAL's Proposal (#5)

Chapter One

Remy LaDue stuck his key in the lock and twisted, pushing open the door to the apartment he hadn't see in four months. As he stepped inside, half of SEAL Team 10 2nd Platoon followed. Much as he loved his teammates, he had been hoping for a few quiet moments to himself. Having just completed a mission in the hills of Afghanistan, he was ready for some quiet time to gather his thoughts and plan his next operation: a Valentine's Day date with Mitchell Sanders, the one woman he'd never been able to forget.

"So, what's it going to be tonight? Steak, beer and football? Or are we just going to hit the rack and sleep away the jetlag?" Big Bird flopped his long lanky frame onto the couch in Remy's apartment. Though his own apartment was two doors down, he and most of the team hung out at Remy's, the usual gathering place for 2nd Platoon when they were on leave in Little Creek, Virginia.

"Man, we can't sleep or piss away the night." Dustman crossed his arms over his broad chest, the tattoos on his bulging biceps. "Tomorrow is fuckin' Valentine's Day. We didn't fly halfway around the world to sit at home. Let's go out and find us some women or we'll be dateless on V'Day."

Dustin Ford, aka Dustman, didn't know a stranger. No matter where he went, he always found a willing woman. Partly due to his masculine physique, but more due to his open, outgoing personality. The man could talk a virgin out of her underwear in public. He was truly gifted.

Remy held up a hand. "You guys will have to do without me on this one." He dumped his duffle bag on the floor and shrugged out of his jacket. After the long flight and little sleep, all he wanted at that moment was a hot shower.

"That's right, all you talked about in the hills was getting back here to implement your Valentine's Day backup plan." Irish backhanded him in the belly and turned to the others. "Our man Gator is going after Mitchell."

"I'm not *going* after Mitchell. She and I made a promise that if neither of us had a date come Valentine's Day, we'd go out together. As a favor to Brewsky."

Every man in the room grew still for a moment, a silent tribute to their fallen comrade.

"Amigo, you'll only be disappointed." Nacho broke the spell. "Brewsky's been gone a year. Mitchell's got her another man. With her blond hair and blue eyes, and…" he waved his hands in the shape of a woman's curves. "She's bound to be taken. You might as well throw your towel in the ring."

"Wrong," Remy argued, though he'd been worried about the same thing. She was gorgeous, smart and tough. Any man would be lucky to have her. "We've been in touch by Skype and email. I told her I'd call when I got back. You guys can go without me. I'll join you if things fall through."

"Come on, Big Bird." Swede offered his hand and jerked the big SEAL from his comfortable position on the couch. "Let the man suffer his humiliation in private."

"We'll be at the Naughty Ladies Lounge around ten o'clock tonight." Dustman rubbed his hands together. "Of course, after a thoroughly satisfying meal of steak and baked potatoes slathered in butter, sour cream and bacon bits, chased with a pitcher of beer each."

Irish groaned. "Can a guy have a foodgasm?"

"Beats the hell out of MREs," Fish noted.

"If I never eat another meal ready to eject, it'll be too soon." Nacho hung back as the others trailed out the door. Once everyone had gone, he turned back. "Really, if Mitchell's not available, you should meet up with us. Sucks to be alone on Valentine's Day. If you don't give yourself at least a day of hunting, you won't have a date for the big day."

"Thanks, Sanchez. I'll keep that in mind. Now…" He gave the man a pointed look.

"I get it. You'd like to call in private." Cesar Sanchez, the compact Hispanic member of their team with dark hair and broad shoulders, backed out the doorway and closed it quietly behind him.

Remy sighed. This moment was the first time that day he'd been alone. Hell, it felt like the first time in months he'd been by himself. His pulse picked up and he grabbed his cell phone, hitting the saved number for Mitchell Sanders. His best friend, Derek

Brewer's girl. A stab of sadness with a chaser of guilt always accompanied any contact with Mitchell.

While Derek had been dating Mitchell, Remy had fallen for the strong-willed, beautiful NCIS agent. Had she been dating anyone else in the world besides one of his teammates, he'd have gone after her and to hell with the guy.

But among his teammates, there was a code of honor. SEALs didn't poach on another SEAL's girl. The last mission Gator and Brewsky had been on together went south. The intel they'd gotten had been faulty to the point Gator suspected it was a ruse to gain their trust long enough to blow them away.

That ruse had cost the lives of three of their platoon. Brewsky, when he threw himself over a grenade during a village sweep. Two other men from their team had been gunned down by the reported "unarmed" villagers. The rest of the team had to pull out and regroup before they could return and mop up the insurgent mess.

Remy waited for the phone to ring on the other end, his mind going back to Brewer's funeral. Mitchell had been there, dressed in a black dress, something she rarely wore, and carrying a single red rose. After the eulogy was given and the coffin lowered into the ground, she tossed in the red rose. At that moment, the tears she'd held back released.

Remy had gathered her in his arms, never able to stand the sight of a woman in tears. Especially when that woman was Mitchell. She'd always been more of a tomboy. Her career with NCIS had been her focus, and she'd told them both that she had a lot she wished to accomplish before she settled down. Maybe she never would.

As SEALs, they understood the sacrifices people made to the greater good of others. Remy also knew that if you didn't take the time to grieve, the raw emotion would come out in other ways. So he let her cry on his shoulder.

That night she'd asked him to stay with her. She hadn't wanted to be alone. In love with her and hurting for the loss of his friend, he couldn't have left had he wanted to. What started out as holding her while she cried changed. Soon, they were tearing at each other's clothing in a desperate attempt to assuage their mutual loss.

He'd made love with Mitchell. God, it was the most beautiful experience of his life. When the passion ebbed, he'd lain with her in his arms for a long time. At first, he'd thought she was asleep. When she finally spoke, she'd voiced his own thoughts.

"That wasn't right." She pushed to a sitting position, wrapping the sheet around her body. "We shouldn't have done it."

He'd sat up beside her and reached out to take her into his arms and tell her everything would be all right. But he couldn't. The guilt crushed him. "What do we do, now?" he'd asked.

Her eyes awash with tears, she said, "You have to go."

He'd nodded, got out of bed, dressed and grabbed his keys. Still, he couldn't leave her like that. "Just so you know, I don't regret making love to you."

Shaking her head, she pressed her hands over her ears. "It was wrong, so wrong. Derek's dead. We were just at his goddamn funeral."

Remy pulled her hands away from her ears. "Look at me," he said in a quiet but stern tone. "I don't regret what we did, just the timing. You're right. The timing was wrong. We both loved Derek. We were both hurting. Don't hate me for needing comfort."

She'd stared up at him, tears clouding her blue eyes. "I don't hate you." Her bottom lip trembled. "I hate myself for letting this happen."

"No, baby." He sat beside her and pulled her into his arms, running a hand over her smooth back. "Don't beat yourself up. Give yourself time."

Time.

Over a year had passed. He'd kept in touch with Mitchell through email, texting and Skype, depending on where he was in the world. He'd been deployed several times and she'd been busy with her work with the NCIS at the Norfolk, Virginia, field office.

They'd grown closer in some ways by talking through their texts and emails. But they hadn't actually seen each other since the night of Derek's funeral. But that was all about to change.

In their last email, they'd agreed that if neither had a date on Valentine's Day, they would not spend it alone.

Remy's gut had been in knots since that message over two weeks ago. They'd been apart long enough for the grief of losing Derek to subside, and the guilt of having made love the night of his funeral had faded.

To Remy, a lot rode on this "date". He'd been in love with Mitchell since before Brewsky died. That love had only grown stronger over the past year of separation.

His heart twisted as the phone rang on the other end. He counted five rings before voicemail picked up.

"Hi, this is Mitchell. I'm not available right now. Leave a message and I'll get back to you as soon as possible."

"Mitchell, it's Remy." He had to clear his throat, it was so tight. "I just got back in town. Tomorrow is Valentine's Day and I don't have a date. Call me."

As he hung up, he worried his message sounded too pathetic. Too late to change it. The message was on her voicemail whether he liked it or not. Now all he had to do was wait for her call.

For the next five minutes, he jumped at every sound, finally realizing he was being ridiculous. She probably had to work late at the office and she'd call him as soon as she could.

Rather than hover over his cell phone, he'd be better off grabbing a shower. If she wanted to meet that night, he wanted to be available.

Setting his cell phone on the counter in the bathroom, he turned the faucet handle to warm, stripped and climbed into the shower. Heaven was warm water and water pressure. After a good fifteen-minute soak under the pulsing showerhead, he turned off the water and stepped out onto the bathmat to check his phone.

No call.

Afraid she might leave her office and eat on her way home, he dialed her office number. Her phone rang seven times, before it rolled over to the operator.

"How may I direct your call?"

"This is Navy SEAL Lieutenant Remy LaDue. I'm trying to reach Mitchell Sanders, but she's not answering. Could you connect me to her supervisor, Barry White?"

"Yes, sir."

Her supervisor answered on the first ring. "White speaking."

"Barry, Remy LaDue. I'm in country and was trying to get hold of Mitchell."

"You and me both, buddy." Her boss paused. "She walked in a couple days ago and requested emergency leave. I granted it and haven't heard a word from her since. You haven't either?"

"No." A twinge of unease knotted his belly. "Last time I heard from her was two weeks ago. We've been downrange until twenty-four hours ago when we flew back to the States."

"Sorry. A friend of hers went missing, and she wanted to take time off to be with the family. Or so she said. I checked; her friend didn't have any family that we know of."

"I see." The knot in Remy's gut tightened, disappointment and concern washing over him. If she hadn't been in contact with her supervisor, she probably wouldn't be calling him anytime soon.

Remy almost decided to order out pizza and stay at his apartment for the night. At the last minute, he changed his mind, threw on a shirt and jeans and hurried out the door to catch his teammates. Steak sounded better than pizza. He set his phone on vibrate and put it in his pocket. If Mitchell called, he'd feel it.

Mitchell adjusted the skimpy costume. The sequined bra barely covered her breasts and the leotard with more decorative holes than fabric stretched over her shoulders and ass so tightly she was afraid one bad move and the holes designed into the costume would join each other, and the entire leotard would pop off her like a giant rubber band. Wincing, she plucked the back out of her butt crack.

"Honey, let it ride. The smaller the costume, the bigger the tips." Dixie Lee adjusted her leopard-print G-string so that the triangle covered her Brazilian bikini wax and tucked her size triple-D boobs into the tight-fitting matching bikini top. Patent leather high heels completed her outfit. With makeup caked on her face to cover the fine lines that too much liquor, drugs and smoking had etched into her skin, she was ready to take her turn on the stage.

Mitchell swallowed hard to keep her nerves from getting the better of her.

The music came to an end on the stage. Men whistled and hooted, yelling for more when Candi pranced in, plucking the dollar bills from her bra and

G-string. "The men are horny tonight, ladies. A whole group of military guys just walked in, fresh from deployment with fistfuls of cash. Who's up?"

"Who do you suggest, Candi?" A gravelly male voice sounded from the backstage door. Rocco Hatch, the bar owner, entered, wearing a black suit jacket over a black shirt and black trousers. His dark hair was slicked back with enough product to make him the envy of most women, and he wore enough cologne to make Mitchell gag.

The man wasn't very tall—maybe five feet nine inches. But, his ego was bigger than the floor space of the bar. He strolled through the strippers, his hand sliding over a breast here, an ass there until he came to a halt beside Candi.

She sneered at the others and draped an arm over Rocco's shoulder, rubbing her breasts against his suit. "I think you should send the new bitch out there, Rocco baby." She pressed her lips to his neck and slid her hand into his suit jacket.

Rocco's brows rose and he directed his stare to Mitchell. "CC? It's a full house out there. Think you've got what it takes to keep their attention?"

Mitchell pushed back her dread, reminding herself that this was the man with the connections. If she wanted to find Kelli, she'd have to play his game. Plumping her breasts, she let her eyelids drift low and her lips curl up slightly on the corners, striving for a confidence she wasn't feeling. Though she loved to dance, she'd never pole danced or stripped in public. Her stomach clenched. If she wasn't good enough, the customers would eat her alive and she'd lose her chance of capturing the boss's attention.

"I've got it." Using the steps she'd practiced in front of her mirror at home, she vamped her way through the other ladies in the dressing room and stopped in front of Rocco, gave Candi a brief, dismissive glance and walked her fingers up Rocco's chest. "You won't be disappointed." Leaning forward, she gave him an eyeful of cleavage.

His nostrils flared.

Candi's eyes narrowed and her hand slid down Rocco's belly to caress his member that had swelled beneath his zipper. "Go on, then. Let's see what you have."

Mitchell winked at Rocco and stepped out on the stage. The bright lights blinded her, shining up into her eyes. She counted them as a blessing. What she couldn't see couldn't hurt her, could it? Hopefully, she wouldn't spot anyone she knew out there.

As she danced across the stage, Robin Thicke's song *Blurred Lines* blasted through the speakers. Hesitant at first, Mitchell stared out at the crowd, glad she couldn't see the individual faces. But this dance really wasn't for them. She'd convinced Rocco that she was a professional club dancer and she could hold her own on the dance floor. If she wanted to remain in the bar and get closer to Rocco, she had to put her money where her mouth was and dance.

Pushing back her shoulders, she strutted across to center stage where a pole stretched from floor to ceiling. She wrapped both hands around the pole and dropped to her haunches, her knees flaring out on either side of the hard metal, her pelvis pumping in rhythm to the song.

Hoots from the men in the audience emboldened her and she raised her hips, her hands low on the pole until her ass stuck up in the air, her butt cheeks probably glistening in the lighting with all the glitter she'd sprinkled over them. Straightening, she wrapped a leg around the pole and leaned back, giving them a good flash of boobs.

More hooting and dollars flew onto the stage.

She spun, dropped her leg and arched her back to the pole, dropping into a squat, her knees wide, giving the men a good view of her crotch. This display of blatant sexuality for money made her skin crawl. It went against everything she'd worked so hard to overcome in her life. As an NCIS agent, she'd taken all kinds of crap from men. But this undercover operation was completely off the books. Even Barry didn't know what she was attempting.

And she wouldn't be doing it, if they'd assigned a better agent to investigate Lt. Kelli O'Neal's disappearance.

Kelli had been her friend and roommate when Mitchell went through the Naval Academy. Though they'd gone their separate ways after graduation, they'd kept in touch.

Mitchell completed her four years' active duty and had taken a position with NCIS, gone to Quantico for training, and had been assigned to the Little Creek field office.

When Kelli had gotten orders for Norfolk Naval Base, Mitchell had been happy to see her friend move to the area. The timing couldn't have been better.

She'd come two months after Derek's death and had helped her through the grief of Derek's loss, and her guilt over sleeping with his best friend the night of Derek's funeral.

Then two weeks ago, Kelli disappeared. Vanished. She'd been reported AWOL from her duty station and NCIS had been contacted to conduct the investigation. Because Mitchell was a close friend, the case had gone to Brendan Wallace.

Mitchell hadn't been satisfied with how slow he was moving. The longer Kelli was missing, the lower the chance of them finding her. After numerous attempts to get Brendan to work faster, she'd gone to Barry and asked him to oversee the investigation personally. He'd stepped in all right. But he'd told her she was interfering with the case, and if she didn't back off, he'd put her on administrative leave.

Knowing she was too close to the victim, Mitchell couldn't help feeling Brendan wasn't looking at the case from the right angle. She'd gotten into the files and reviewed the witness testimony and none of the statements added up.

As far as she was concerned, time was running out for Kelli. If she didn't do something soon, her friend might be lost forever, maybe even dead. So she'd asked for leave and started her own investigation.

Which led to this bar. A bar Kelli would never have stepped foot into—at least, willingly. But the man Kelli had been seeing just happened to own it—Rocco Hatch.

Mitchell glanced to where she'd left the man

standing backstage. Rocco wasn't there. She rose to her feet, swiveled her hips and rocked them, suggestively soliciting more wolf calls and dozens of hands in the air waving dollar bills.

Rocco stood at the bar, away from the frenetic shouts of the young men lining the stage. He expected her to act like a stripper. To get close enough for the men to stuff money into the strings holding up her bottoms and into the bra of her top.

She was glad for the leggings, even if they had holes all the way up her thighs and over her hips; the garment gave the men more places to tuck money. The crisscrossing strings holding her leotard together at the front also held her bra in place. No one could easily rip it off her and she wouldn't be expected to strip all the way down to nothing. When applying for the job, she'd emphasized she was a dancer. "I don't take off my clothes in public," she'd said and winked. "I save that for the privacy of a bedroom."

To prove that fact to Rocco, she danced toward the edge of the stage, turned and dropped to her haunches, exposing her bottom to the nearest men. Hands groped her ass and tucked money anywhere they could.

Fighting to keep from slugging them, she pretended to enjoy the attention and straightened as soon as she could without looking as if she was running away. Before she could walk back to center stage, she felt big hands grab her hips and drag her backward.

A gasp escaped. She teetered on her heels, lost her balance and felt herself falling into the sea of male faces.

Young men, short haircuts, and bulging muscles spelled military. And all yelling at once, all horny, all groping for their ounce of flesh.

"Hey, baby, over here."

"I could use some of that."

"Whew, mamma. That's what I'm talking about!"

One voice stood out among the rest.

"Mitchell?" Navy SEAL Remy LaDue's face swam into view before she was lifted and slammed into the broad wall of a chest belonging to a man who could have wrestled gorillas at the local zoo. He leered down at her and reached for one of her breasts.

A fist flew at his jaw and landed with a bone-rattling thud. The ape barely reacted, his hand grabbing a handful of her right boob and squeezing hard.

Mitchell fought to get her feet under her while prying at the massive paw clutching her. "Let go of me," she demanded.

"Finders keepers," the big guy said, his voice deep enough to lead ships through foggy waters.

Based on his long hair and big gut, he wasn't one of the military men.

Mitchell bit her lip. Military men, she could handle. But a big, hulking redneck, now that was another situation entirely.

"The lady asked you to let go," Remy's voice sounded above the noise of the crowd.

"I will, when I'm good and ready." The gorilla grinned stupidly and squeezed her like a stress ball. "I'm not ready."

"Let her dance," a man shouted behind him.

"Yeah, let her dance," another sailor yelled.

The room erupted in a chant of "Let her dance!"

Rocco's bouncers muscled their way through the crowd of men. Before they could reach her, Remy kicked the gorilla in the knee. The man loosened his hold long enough for Mitchell to get away. With the help of the men in the crowd, she was lifted back up on the stage, a few dollars heavier and with a bruised breast.

The music switched to the Katy Perry song, *Peacock*.

A group of men lifted Remy out of the crowd as well and handed him up on edge of the stage in a straight back chair. The chant started again, with "Lap dance!" Soon, the entire club had taken up the chant.

Remy sat in the chair, his brows drawn together in a severe frown. Every time he tried to rise from the chair, someone jerked him back onto his butt.

"What the hell are you doing here?" he shouted over the music.

Mitchell shot a glance to the point she'd last seen Rocco. His brows had dipped as low as Remy's and he was following the bouncers through the crowd, making little headway among the rowdy SEALs.

Knowing she only had a moment to get her message across, she danced over to Remy, straddled his legs and gave him the lap dance the men demanded. She leaned forward, shaking her breasts in his face. "Grab my ass. Look like you're enjoying it, for Pete's sake!"

She smiled and rubbed her breasts across his

face, then bent to nibble at his ear and said in a voice only Remy could hear, "You don't know me. I'm undercover here. Don't make a scene."

When she started to get up, she felt him grab her hips and hold her in his lap. *That's the spirit.* Mitchell winked at him and ground her bottom against his groin, pretending to ride him like a stallion. "Yeehaw!" When she bent forward, she whispered, "Please, don't blow my cover."

Remy said with a low growl, "I won't stand by and let someone maul you."

"At least look like you're having fun, damn it." She arched her back and let her long curly hair drape down over his knees.

A second later, Remy buried his face in her cleavage while gripping her bottom.

Heat flared between her legs, her crotch grinding against the hardness of his erection. God, it had been too long since she'd made love to a man. Too long.

As his head came up, he smiled, his gaze direct and intense. "Meet me at the back door when you get off work."

By that time, Rocco and the bouncers had pushed through the men and climbed up on the stage.

With a flippant smile, she winked. "It'll cost you, baby." Mitchell rose, turned and bent to touch her toes, shining her bottom in Remy's face before dancing away. She trailed her fingers across the first bouncer's chest and paused at Rocco, cupping his cheek. Then she patted it, forced a sultry smile and returned to center stage where she hooked her leg around the pole, and arched her back, her arms above her head, her gaze following Remy off the stage.

Holy shit!

She'd come so close to blowing everything she'd worked for the past twenty-four hours.

Though joy surged at Remy's reappearance after more than a year, dread tempered her happiness. If he knew what she was up to, he'd go all macho and refuse to let her go through with her plan. She had to talk to him. But she knew she was being watched and Rocco would be close, following her every move. The man hadn't gotten away with the horrible things he'd done by being careless.

Other Titles by Elle James

Other Titles by Elle James

Devil's Shroud/Deadly Series
Deadly Reckoning (#1)
Deadly Engagement(#2)
Deadly Liaisons(#3)
Deadly Allure(#4)
Stealth Operations Specialists Series
Blown Away
Alaskan Fantasy
Nick of Time
Others
Beneath the Texas Moon
Dakota Meltdown
Lakota Baby
Cowboy Sanctuary
Texas-Sized Secrets
Under Suspicion, with Child
Baby Bling
An Unexpected Clue
Operation XOXO
Killer Body
Bundle of Trouble
Haunted
Time Raiders: The Whisper
Cowboy Brigade
Engaged with the Boss
Tarzan & Janine
The Billionaire Husband Test

CPSIA information can be obtained at www.ICGtesting.com
Printed in the USA
BVOW06s0150020416

442722BV00021B/134/P